A Winter Garden Blossom

Douglas Lim

Inscript

Bladensburg, MD

Published by Inscript Books
a division of Dove Christian Publishers
P.O. Box 611
Bladensburg, MD 20710-0611
www.inscriptpublishing.com

Inscript and the portrayal of a pen with script are trademarks of Dove Christian Publishers.

Book Design by Mark Yearnings

ISBN: 978-1-7375177-6-4

Printed in the United States of America

*To Daughter and all girls whose hearts shine
with God's love
and goodness before others*

Chapter 1

I hated making new friends at school every time we moved. "How many times have I changed schools, Mom?"

She laughed. "Five times, darling. How can I forget? You remind me just about every other day."

I nodded. "I'm just checking. I don't want you to forget."

"Sydney, please grab the shovel over in the corner and help me dig three holes to plant my new batches of roses."

For as long as I can remember, Mom loved gardening. But since we moved so much the past few years, she couldn't have a garden in the backyard. Mom enjoyed escaping into her world of flowers and vegetables so much. She often spent the entire weekend working her plot of land, always looking for ways to spruce it up, which she liked to call her paradise getaway.

"Mom, do you remember the garden you planted inside one of our tiny apartments we moved into?"

She shook her head. "Please don't remind me. Terrible idea." Mom missed gardening so much she planted a vegetable garden in the apartment. But we didn't stay long enough for us to see how the experiment turned out.

"Sorry for bringing it up, Mom."

She grinned. "What a whirlwind the past few years have been for all of us, moving from city to city, apartment to apartment, school to school."

The days of packing and unpacking were over. Having our own house again with a big backyard for gardening was a dream come true, especially for Mom. She could get just about anything in the ground to grow. God gave her a green thumb for sure. Everyone knew where we could find her on the weekends.

I grabbed the shovel, throwing it over my shoulder. "Mom, I have the shovel. We should plant the roses in front of the breakfast room window, so when they bloom, you can admire them as you have breakfast."

Mom smiled. "That's a great idea. The roses will get lots of sunshine all day from there. I'll get the wheelbarrow to move the dirt we dig out for later use."

"Can I start digging, Mom?"

"Sure. But please put your hat on and apply sunscreen before you start, Sydney."

The sun glistered off the sweat on Mom's face. I worked up a sweat, too. It was only the middle of spring, but the temperature read 85 degrees on the wall thermometer. I didn't enjoy gardening that much, but I liked hanging around with Mom, chatting about things as she tilled the soil.

After school, I would sometimes sit on the patio by myself, staring at the rainbow of colors glimmering from the squash, tomatoes, bell peppers, lettuce, and cucumbers in the garden. It helped me to relax after a tiring day at school. We had a lemon tree—great for homemade lemonade during the hot summer days. Mom's plans included an orange tree and a garden pond next to the patio.

"I'm so happy we're here to stay, Mom. I didn't realize how much I missed living in our own house, with our very own backyard, until we moved here. We not moving again, right?"

Mom dragged a bag of compost closer to the flower bed where we were planting the roses. "Darling, as I mentioned to you many times, we're not moving again. Please stop worrying."

I tapped Mom's shoulder. "Is that a promise?"

She squinted against the sun as she looked up at me. "All I can tell you is we have no plans to move anytime soon."

I thanked God every day for keeping us safe and giving my parents a job so we could stay here for a long time. At least I knew I would finish my last two years of middle school at Winter Garden and probably high school without having to move again.

Mom never complained to us much about moving, but I never kept it a secret how it affected me, which Dad knew all too well. "Yikes! I see cobwebs, Mom. Better get the bug spray just in case Mr. Spider makes a mad dash for me."

"Be careful, darling. Don't get the spray all over yourself. It's windy."

Mom's face beamed with joy the first day we moved to this house. She couldn't stop talking about her plans to transform our backyard into a paradise. She stared out across her new backyard with her arms outstretched over her head, thanking God. I noticed a few happy tears, too. She missed pruning, watering, and all the other gardening activities so much.

"Mom, is this deep enough for the roses? I tried to make it about a foot deep."

"If you can make the holes a little deeper, we should be good to go. You're a big help, darling."

I noticed Dad peeking out the door. "Hey, Dad. We can use some help. Come join us back here."

He grinned. "It looks like you guys have everything under

control. Besides, I have a game I want to finish watching. Sorry, it's a close one." He disappeared back inside the house.

Dad had a hard time finding work back when we moved all the time. I often heard my parents talking about people losing their jobs and hoping life would get better soon. Whenever we moved to another town, Dad made sure we lived in a safe place and didn't have to worry about putting food on the table. He also wanted us to dress nicely for school and church.

I struggled to make the holes deeper. "Are things better for Uncle Charles and Aunt Mary?"

Mom grinned. "Yes, they got their jobs back, thank goodness. Darling, I know you experienced many difficulties too. But our situation is much better now. Let's be grateful."

Having to sell our old house hit Dad hard—probably worse than losing the job he worked for over 15 years. He spent a lot of time alone after it happened, staring at the television for hours sometimes. He promised to get us another house as soon as possible. My uncle and aunt would come by from time to time to borrow money and food. A lot of family friends lost their jobs, too. Dad reminded us to pray for our friends, the economy to get better, and all our relatives.

Every time I made a few friends at school, we ended up packing and moving again. I didn't know if making friends was worth the pain of having to say goodbye. "Mom, could you check the hole for the roses again? It looks deep enough to me."

She stuck a ruler in the hole. "Perfect. Time for a break, darling. I think we deserve one."

"I'm always ready for a break." I dusted my hands against my jeans and picked off a few leaves stuck to my hat.

I became a worrier. Even with high school years away, I

already wondered if someone would invite me to the senior prom. I exercised like crazy and starved myself sometimes, and the next minute, I found myself binge eating. Those moving days had to be the worst days of my life.

Mom slipped off her shoes and went inside. "It's hot today. Let me get a washcloth so we can wipe our faces."

Mom worried about me having to adjust to a new school all the time. I hated introducing myself and seeing those forced smiles and stares all day. For some reason, no one ever asked me to join them for lunch. But I kept hoping and praying the hard times would go away one day.

I grabbed the washcloth, flopping it on my face. "It feels great, refreshing as can be."

School life got awful sometimes. I could deal with the students ignoring me and even the eye rolls, but some of the students were plain rude. And having to use a map to find my classrooms the first few days sure made it easy for others to poke fun at me.

"I think we did a good job so far," said Mom. "I love your idea for the roses. I can almost picture them blossoming in my head."

"Really?"

Mom poured a cup of coffee and sank into her favorite chair in the kitchen, staring out the window as she sipped. It was quiet except for the humming of the refrigerator. Mom seemed lost in thought.

"Are you resting, Mom?"

"Sorry. How is everything going at school?" Mom's eyes still focused on the roses we planted. Having friends at school and a place we could finally call home was a relief for her.

"I'm getting pretty good grades on my tests and homework assignments. By the way, we have a science project in Mrs.

Clark's class. It's a group project. Michelle and I are working on it together, but we need to find a couple of other classmates to join our group."

"When is it due?" said Mom. "I hope Michelle and her parents are doing well."

"It's an end-of-semester project. Michelle's parents seem fine. They're always nice to me. Thanks for letting me go over to study with Michelle. She's always so much fun."

Mom hesitated. "I hope you guys aren't having too much fun that you don't finish your homework."

"Nope. We always finish our homework. Michelle is good about getting her homework done."

Mom grinned. "I'm sure glad you have such a good friend."

"She is my very first best friend." I thanked God all the time for bringing Michelle into my life.

Mom swung around in her chair and gazed at me. "I know the moving made it hard for you to make good friends. I'm so sorry we had to put you through all the moving."

"Yeah. I'm sorry too for being a teenager monster sometimes. I just got so tired of moving from school to school. I'm glad we're staying for a long while."

Mom sighed. "Me too." We looked at each other and busted out laughing.

"I guess you're happy about getting your garden back."

Mom chuckled. "Is it so obvious to everyone?"

"Yeah, Mom. It's as plain as the nose on your face."

Mom laughed. "You're hanging around Grandma too much. You sound like her more and more every day."

Chapter 2

I fought with Dad the last time we moved. From his low-pitched voice, I knew what he was about to tell me. The news came halfway through the school year, and I had friends I didn't want to leave behind. My heart sank when he broke the bad news about having to move again.

I shouted at Dad. "You're the worse father ever. It's not fair what you're doing to me." I had never been so disrespectful to him before.

"I'm sorry." Dad reached out to hug me. I pulled away from him.

"Why can't you be like everyone else's dad? If I get married and have kids, I will never do this to them."

He tried to explain. Not wanting to hear his speech about how things would get better soon, I cut him off.

Dad twisted his hands together. "I'm so sorry, darling. We have to get ready to move in a few weeks."

Tears filled my eyes as I stared at Dad. "You have to do something so we can stay. You can't do this to me again. It's not fair."

"I know. I know. It's been so hard finding steady work," said Dad. "I tried looking everywhere. I hope you'll forgive me."

"Never. Leave me alone," I shouted, stomping my feet. "I can't believe you would do this to me."

Dad didn't say another word and plodded out of the room. I slammed the door behind him and began flinging shoes and clothes everywhere. "Darling, are you all right?" whispered Mom behind the door.

"No, I'm not all right. Please leave me alone." I heard Mom's steps as she headed down the hall. Grabbing my pillow to my face, I screamed as hard as I could.

I pleaded to God. *"How come this is happening to me? I don't understand why I have to go through this again. You gave me friends, and now you're taking them away from me. I don't understand."*

* * *

Tired from crying on and off most of the night, I overslept. Shuffling of boxes could be heard coming from Mom's room. In the kitchen, I saw boxes already filled with pots and pans and cups and dishes.

Grandma stood ready in the kitchen. "Good morning, darling. I'll warm up your breakfast unless you want lunch instead."

I assumed she had heard about what happened the night before. "I'll have breakfast. Sorry for being late. I can't believe we're moving again."

Grandma tapped me on the shoulder and sighed. "Well, I know your father is doing the best he can. What do you want on your toast today?"

"Strawberry jam, Grandma. I've been at this school for a whole semester. How can this be happening again? I like my friends so much." A semester was just long enough to get comfortable and have a few close friends. I even joined a club.

Grandma wrapped her arm around my shoulder. "One semester is quite a long time for you. I know it's going to make leaving hard. I made friends I'm going to miss, too. I'm so sorry, darling."

After breakfast, Grandma read the Bible to me. She recited a few verses that snapped me out of my lousy mood and gave me hope. Grandma knew how to explain the Bible, making sure I understood what God wanted to tell me. She became my escape from all the hurts and disappointments, especially the loneliness I experienced from all the years of moving.

"I want a normal life with friends, and I hate worrying about being the new kid at school all the time. I've lost hope, Grandma."

She nodded. "Like all difficult times in our lives, God reminds us that all these things shall pass. He has never failed to keep His word. Darling, ask God to help you with your anger toward your dad and also to give you faith that your school situation will get better soon."

I couldn't have gotten through the moving and drama at all the different schools the last few years without Grandma. She knew what I needed to hear from her. "It's getting harder and harder each time we move."

Grandma smiled. "Let's finish our breakfast, and after I wash the dishes, we can take a stroll around the neighborhood and talk some more."

"I'll help you clean up, Grandma. Let me dry the dishes for you, and I'll put them away, too."

Every time we moved, my relationship with Dad got worse. Arguing with Dad became routine. Sometimes, I wouldn't talk to him for weeks.

* * *

I didn't know how to break the news to my friends and thought about writing them a letter so I wouldn't have to face them. But I decided to tell them at lunchtime instead. "Hey, guys. I got some bad news to tell you. My parents told me we're moving in a few weeks. I'm not handling it very well."

My friend Mary jumped up from her seat. "What? You can't leave us." The bell rang. Everyone dumped their trash and raced off to class. Mary glanced back and shouted, "I'll talk to you later, Sydney."

For some reason, my friends never talked to me about my big announcement afterward. A week went by, and I wondered if they even cared.

As I waited for the bus, Mary came over and reminded me about coming to her house that night. "Sydney, you're still coming over to do homework, right? I need your help with math class again."

I nodded. "Sure. I won't forget. I'll be over around the usual time." When I got home, I locked myself in my room, feeling sorry for myself. Life seemed so gloomy and heavy.

"It's getting late, darling. Are you still going over to Mary's house to do homework?" asked Mom. "You guys normally get together on Wednesdays. I hope you didn't forget all about it."

"No, Mom. I'm still going. I'm just a little late."

When I got to Mary's house, I knocked and knocked again. Since the lights were off inside the house, I turned to leave, then the door opened.

"Surprise!" my friends screamed out. They crawled out from under the table and popped up from behind an old couch in the living room. Purple and pink balloons, my favorite colors, decorated the room. Mary's mom even came out and hugged me.

She thanked me for helping Mary with her homework and told me how much she would miss me.

I grabbed Mary's arm and whispered, "I had no idea."

Mary laughed. "I hope you didn't think we forgot all about you leaving us. We wanted to surprise you. We have cake and a gift for you, too."

"I guess we're not doing homework tonight," I smirked, pumping my fist in the air.

"We're not," said Mary. "Let's get the party going."

We talked all night about the fun things we enjoyed together—watching cartoons on movie night, window shopping, getting manicures, and baking cookies. And we danced and sang along to our favorite songs.

"I loved the chocolate-covered chips and cake. I want you to know you're the best friends I've ever had. You've taught me so much about friendship and kindness. I will miss you so much. Sorry for blubbering all over you. Love you guys." My friends gave me a friendship bracelet they made themselves for my going-away present.

I never got over the scariness of moving to a new school. My insides knotted up at the thought of not knowing a single person, and I worried too much about what others thought about me. Hearing the whispers as I walked by students in the hallway and getting left out of activities all the time made school life miserable.

It's funny how being alone at a new school all the time changed how I saw students like myself. I became aware of the students who sat by themselves at lunch with no one to talk to, who buried themselves in the library day after day as I sometimes did, who got pushed around for just being new at school.

Chapter 3

Mom shouted from downstairs. "Sydney, please hurry down. I don't want you guys to be late for school again. Your brother and I will wait for you in the car." A bit of a night owl, I often struggled to get up in time for school.

I stuck my head out the bedroom door. "Will do. I'll be down in a minute, Mom." I stared into the mirror yet again. Something didn't seem right with my shoes. Kicking them off, I hunted down another pair.

My brother grew impatient, screaming from Mom's car. "Hurry up, Sydney. I don't want to be late and have to stay after school because of you."

Peeking out the window, I saw Mom pushing my brother's hands away from the car horn. I gave myself another look-over to make sure my color choices made sense and rushed downstairs, stopping at the bottom to check my backpack. "Mom, wait one more second. I forgot my mirror."

Mom glanced back as I tossed my backpack into the car and jumped in. "It looks like we're finally ready to go," said Mom. "Please buckle your seat belts."

My brother grumbled. "I have to get to school on time—can't afford to be late again."

Mom nodded. "We're going to make it. I'll take the shortcut.

Keep your fingers crossed." Mom weaved through the traffic, avoiding the red lights.

"Now there's a car in front of us who refuses to turn," said my brother. He reached for the horn.

Mom stared at him. "Don't touch the horn. Relax! I'll get you to school on time."

I pulled out my mirror and checked my hair and makeup. I was insecure about so many things—my classmates' opinions about me, my clothes, and my ever-changing body.

Mom decelerated into the school parking lot and dropped me off by the back entrance. "Have a good day. I'll see you tonight."

"Bye, Mom. Thank you for getting me to school on time."

Mom stuck her head out the window. "Michelle, say hello to your mom for me."

Michelle walked over to me, smiling. "You're going to the dance with me, right? I guarantee you'll have fun there. You have nothing to worry about." She'd been asking me for weeks.

I shrugged. "Well, I haven't decided yet."

Michelle huffed. "Tell me you're kidding."

I had little to complain about compared to all the drama I dealt with the last few years. I had the best friend in the world to hang around with, good pals to eat and laugh at lunchtime, and I got good grades. One of my friends even attended the same church as me.

"What can I do to convince you to go?" asked Michelle. "It's not a big deal, Sydney."

"Well, you know me."

Michelle shook her head. "Come on, don't tell me it's your looks again."

"Yeah. That's part of it." I had first-dance jitters for sure and didn't have a clue about how to deal with it.

Michelle smiled. "You look great all the time, and I always like the clothing choices you make."

"I appreciate your compliments, Michelle. You're a real boost to my confidence."

Michelle looked me over. "Your outfit, hair, shoes, makeup choices always make good fashion sense to me."

"Thank you. I have gotten over some of my insecurities, but feeling like I'm not good enough isn't one of them."

Michelle nodded. "Aww, it must be hard for you. I'm sorry for being so pushy."

"Suppose I get all dolled up and end up standing in a corner by myself. Suppose I get a zit on my nose. Suppose I trip on the dance floor in front of everyone."

Michelle tapped my shoulder. "I know that won't happen. Your imagination is just getting haywire."

"I promise to let you know tomorrow. You're the best." A twinge of guilt crept in. I owed her a decision.

Michelle sighed. "I've been waiting almost a month. I guess I can wait one more day. You promised me a decision."

I glanced at my watch. "We better get going. I have to stop by my locker before class."

Michelle nodded. "Me too. We better run."

We raced past the students still loitering around the hallway, busting through the classroom door just as the bell rang. Mrs. Clark was writing our homework assignment on the board. I sat as still as possible, so it didn't look like I just rushed in.

Mrs. Clark glanced over at Michelle and me. "Good morning. It looks like everyone is here on time today. Next time we're running late, let's not smash through the door. I don't want to have to call maintenance to repair the door hinges again."

I wondered why I thought Mrs. Clark wouldn't notice. She practically had eyes behind her head. "Let's pass our homework in and start our lesson for today. Sydney and Michelle, please help collect the homework. Thank you."

I glanced over at Michelle, and a grin flashed across her face. "Yes, Mrs. Clark. We'll take care of it."

Mrs. Clark spun around in her chair. "Before I forget, I want to remind you that our annual school dance is right around the corner. If you are planning to attend, please get your tickets early. We want to get an idea of how many will be attending."

Michelle glanced over at me, giving me a thumbs-up. The decision of whether or not to go to the dance weighed heavily on my shoulders all day.

Chapter 4

Michelle deserved an answer. I couldn't weasel out of it any longer. Grandma taught me never to rush into a decision without praying first, especially something like whether or not to go to the dance.

"I'm back, Grandma." She shuffled over and gave me a quick hug, returning to whisking her bowl of egg whites.

"How did your day go at school, darling?" She always had something for me to eat after school. The rattling of her favorite cooking pan and the smell of the bread browning in the toaster told me it was almost time to eat.

"Sit down, darling. Your eggs will be ready in a few minutes." I shoved my backpack into the closet and scrubbed up. Grandma usually sat with me as I ate and listened to whatever I wanted to talk about—and cheered me up if I had a terrible day.

Grandma sprinkled nuts and parmesan cheese on my scrambled eggs as I took a sip of my strawberry smoothie. I never thought healthy food could taste so good.

"Would you like some yogurt?"

"No, thank you. Remember the school dance I told you about, Grandma. Well, Michelle is still waiting for my decision. I've been putting it off. It's not nice to keep Michelle waiting, but I still feel nervous about going."

Grandma smiled. "Oh, I thought you already told her, darling. Yeah. It's probably good to let her know pretty soon."

"I'm afraid of embarrassing myself if I attend. Suppose I get all dolled up, and all the guys ignore me or even make fun of me? I don't know what I should do."

Grandma scooted her chair next to me. "I'm sorry to hear you feel this way. Sydney, we all have insecurities about different things. By the way, when I was your age, I never thought I looked pretty enough, which made me feel terrible for a long time."

"You never told me this before. But Grandma, from the pictures you showed me, you looked beautiful. It's true."

Grandma laughed. "Thank you, darling. That's sweet of you to say. Finish up your eggs. Dinner won't be for a while."

I gobbled up my scrambled eggs, washing them down with the rest of my smoothie. "Yeah. That's kind of how I feel. I'm always comparing myself to others. My friends tell me how great I look, but I can't stop thinking it's not true."

"You're beautiful, darling. Comparison is a dangerous trap I fell into, too."

"It's dangerous?"

Grandma nodded and wrapped her arms around me. "When we compare ourselves to our friends all the time, even people we don't know very well, it will just make us unhappy. Never forget, God created you beautifully for a good purpose. You're special to Him, and best of all, He never makes mistakes."

"Yeah. It all made sense, but it's still hard to stop caring about what other people think of me."

Grandma grinned. "I know. Let's ask God to help you. I used to pray about my problems every day until things got better."

"Is it all right to ask God to make me skinny and beautiful anyway?"

Mom chuckled. "No, it's not a good idea, darling."

We bowed our heads, and Grandma prayed. "*Lord, please guide Sydney to see things in a better way. Help her to trust in You more, knowing You love her deeply. Let her come to see her special gifts, her beauty, and her unique talents. May she value and use the many skills You have given her. Protect my precious granddaughter and give her the guidance she needs to make the right decision about the school dance. Amen.*"

I smiled. "Amen. Thank you for praying for me, Grandma."

"You're welcome. Darling, can you help me clean up the kitchen and dishes? I'm falling a little behind."

"Sure, no problem."

Grandma suddenly gripped the back of her chair to keep from falling. "Sydney, I'm feeling a little dizzy."

I held on to her and helped her to sit down. "Are you all right? Your hands are cold, Grandma."

"I need to rest for a few minutes. Please get me a glass of water so I can take my medication." Grandma shut her eyes and rested her head in her hands.

"I'll get your medication for you." I headed upstairs to her room.

Grandma called me back. "Sydney, it's in the cabinet next to the sink."

"I found it. Should I call Mom?"

"No. Please hand me my cup of water, darling."

I wiped the water that dripped from her mouth as Grandma took her medication. "Let me help you to your room so you can get some rest. You should lie down."

Grandma grinned. "Good idea. I'm feeling a little better now. Thank you, darling."

I held tight to Grandma's arm, and we climbed upstairs. She sat down on the edge of her bed. I pulled her slippers off and helped her crawl under the covers.

"Hope you're feeling better. I'll stay with you for a while."

"I'm fine, darling." Grandma grabbed my hand and thanked me. Her hands felt a lot warmer. After a few minutes, she dozed off. I went downstairs to clean up the kitchen before Mom came home from work.

As I finished putting the last dish away, I heard mom's car pull into the driveway. "Hi, Mom."

Mom slipped on her house shoes and stared at me. "Why are you wearing Grandma's apron?"

"I'm helping her clean up the kitchen. She got a little dizzy."

"What happened, darling?" shouted Mom, dropping her purse and keys on the kitchen counter. "Where is she now?"

"Grandma is sleeping in her room."

"I guess I better check on her." Mom raced upstairs.

I went to my room and thought about what Grandma had discussed with me. I was ready to give Michelle my decision.

"Knock, Knock." Mom walked into my room, smiling. She threw her arms around me and squeezed tight. "Grandma told me how you took such good care of her. Thank you, darling. I'll call you when dinner is ready—love you."

"I'm glad she's better, Mom. I'll go see her after I finish my homework."

Chapter 5

Mom turned into the school parking lot and dropped me off as usual. "Bye, darling. I'll see you after work. Don't forget to take your jacket."

I was early for school for a change and headed to my morning hangout spot under the oak tree in front of the school. Michelle spotted me coming toward her and glared at me. But as I got closer, a grin flashed across her face.

I laughed. "Why did you give me a silly look?"

Michelle glared at me again. "Hey, you called me late last night and said you finally decided."

I slipped off my backpack and leaned it against the oak tree. "Sorry for calling you so late."

Michelle nudged me in the side. "Yeah. But you didn't tell me your decision and only mentioned you would let me know before class."

"It was late. Besides, I wanted to keep you in suspense."

Michelle wiggled her finger at me. "That's not funny. So, what's your decision?"

"I talked with my grandma, and I feel a lot better about going." Grandma helped me see things in a better way, which took a lot of pressure off me.

Michelle leaned forward. "Great, I'm holding you to this. It's too late to change your mind now."

I smiled. "This is my decision."

Michelle pumped her fist in the air. "Whoopee! We can finally go shopping together and come up with ideas about what to wear. Sydney, it only took you a whole month to make this decision. You sure know how to keep someone in suspense."

"Sorry, I took so long."

We bent over, laughing.

"You know, I'm still pretty nervous about going. I've never been to a dance before. What am I supposed to do—sit on a chair and wait for some strange guy to invite me to dance? Suppose he's creepy, and I don't want to dance with him. Do I tell him to bug off?"

Michelle laughed. "You're my best friend. We'll stick together. Everything is going to be fine. It's not as complicated as you think."

I shrugged, forcing a smile. "All right, if you say so. I trust you."

Michelle leaned in and whispered, "I'm glad you're all right about going to the dance. I hope you don't think I'm forcing you. It's the last thing I want to do."

"Of course not. I thought about it for a long time."

Michelle nodded. "Yeah, I know. Do you want to split my last piece of gum?"

I nodded, taking the gum. "I have no idea what to wear or how to do my hair. I don't know anything."

Michelle grinned. "Sydney, don't you worry your pretty little head. Let's start walking to class. It's getting late. What do you think about Mrs. Clark?"

"She's strict, but Mrs. Clark is one of my favorite teachers for some reason."

Michelle nodded. "I like Mrs. Clark, too. I know she cares about her students. Yeah. But she's such a stickler about rules."

"We better run if we want to make it to class before the bell rings. I don't want to be late for Mrs. Clark's class and have to hear her lecture us about getting to class on time."

I tugged tight the shoulder straps on my backpack. We increased our pace and raced each other across the wet lawn to see who got to class first. Michelle was at least three inches taller than me, which meant she had longer legs. I fell behind right away.

"Michelle, you dropped your pen," I shouted. She stopped and ran back toward me. As Michelle looked for it, I laughed and dashed off.

"Stop! You're cheating."

"I win. I can't believe you fell for it. You're usually not easy to trick."

Michelle shook her head and punched me in the shoulder. "I surprised I fell for it, too. I must be losing my touch."

Michelle knew about my insecurities. I looked up to my best friend. People would tell us that we acted alike. I probably imitated Michelle more than I realized, but no one would ever say we looked anything alike. She stood out from the rest of the girls at school. I've been asking Mom if I could get rid of my eyeglasses. They made me look like someone who worked in the library.

*   *   *

"Please cut out the chatting," said Mrs. Clark. She paused and stared across the classroom. The class went quiet.

Michelle and I had most of our classes together, and lucky for me, I got to sit next to her most of the time, except for Mrs.

Clark's class. I figured Mrs. Clark probably thought we would talk too much. "Sydney and Michelle, could you please pass the books out?" asked Mrs. Clark.

Everyone knew Michelle around school, but she didn't enjoy hanging around the so-call popular girls, which I liked about her. She cared about people, which I needed to learn to do better.

Mrs. Clark tapped on her desk. "All right, let's open our books to chapter five and begin our lesson for today. Thank you for helping with the books, girls."

The teachers would always sit the new students next to Michelle, especially those who were shy or the physically challenged students who needed help fitting in at school. Teachers knew she would be nice and help them make friends. That's how Michelle and I became best friends. She made sure I didn't eat lunch alone.

We celebrated our birthdays together either at my house or her place. Her birthday is one day after mine. I teased her about being my younger sister, even though no one would ever think that.

The bell rang, and I helped collect the books left on top of the students' desks. "Bye, Mrs. Clark. See you tomorrow."

She smiled. "Bye, girls. Thank you again for helping me with the books."

Michelle stared at me. "Do you want to race me to class again? You're going to eat my dust this time."

"Ha-ha. No, I know you'll beat me." Having such a loyal friend made the decision to attend the dance easier for sure.

Chapter 6

Mom peeked inside my room. "I didn't want to disturb you, but it's getting late. Come downstairs for breakfast as soon as you can, darling."

"Mom, the dance is tonight. I need time to make everything perfect." I narrowed my choices down to three outfits but still had my make-up and hair to consider.

Mom smiled. "I know what day it is. You have plenty of time to get ready. I'll see you downstairs in a bit."

I laid my outfits out on the bed and headed down. The more I tried to get everything just right, the more nervous I got. "Where is everyone?"

Mom scrunched her face. "It's 10:30. Everyone finished breakfast, and they're out and about already. Sydney, please relax and have something to eat."

"Sorry for being late. I lost track of time."

"It's all right, darling. I know this is an important day for you. Let me know if you need my help with anything."

"Well, I might want your assistance in choosing the perfect outfit. Michelle told me the dance dress code was casual. I want to make sure I'm not too casual or not casual enough. You know what I mean, Mom?"

"Sure. Just give me a holler. I better finish washing the dishes before it gets too late." Mom grabbed the rest of the dishes off the table and dumped them into the dishpan.

I locked myself in my room the rest of the day, trying on different outfits a couple more times. As far as make-up went, I settled on lip gloss and mascara.

"Come quick! I need your help," I shouted.

Mom rushed up the stairs and stared at me. "What's wrong, Sydney?"

"My favorite lip gloss rolled under the bed somewhere. It vanished into thin air."

Mom shook her head. "Hand me your flashlight. It looks like you have a pair of dusty sneakers under your bed. Wait a minute. I see it. Your precious lip gloss is hiding in the corner. Hold the flashlight while I grab it."

"Thank you, Mom. Sorry for yelling. I wondered where those sneakers went." I put the lip gloss away in my purse. Mom never taught me how to put on make-up. She thought I looked great without it and encouraged me to be confident not wearing any.

"They're here to pick you up for the dance," shouted Mom. "Let's hurry."

I double-checked my hair and make-up and skipped downstairs. "Mom, how does my outfit look? Please, don't tell me something doesn't look quite right."

She smiled. "You look wonderful, darling. Remember to take your scarf. It might get chilly later. Love you. I'll come by around ten o'clock to pick you guys up after the dance. You have everything?"

I looked inside my purse. "I'm didn't forget anything, Mom. Thank you."

She put her hands on my shoulder and looked fondly at me.

"You're shaking, darling. Are you all right? Grandma and I are praying for you. Everything is going to be fine. Have a good time."

Michelle's dad beeped his horn. I dashed out of the house, hopped in the car, and we drove off.

"You two look great," said Michelle's dad. "Is the assistant principal going to be there again this year to watch over things, Michelle?"

"I'm not sure who's going to be there, Dad. Don't worry. They always have a few teachers at the dance supervising us."

"I'll take a peek inside when I drop you guys off."

Michelle cast a glance at me. "I like how you did your make-up and hair, and your outfit looks perfect on you."

"Thank you. I just threw something on. Hey, is the dance usually crowded?"

Michelle laughed. "Not too crowded. I hope they got enough food."

"You're already thinking about food." I stared out the car window and didn't say much during the drive over to the dance.

Michelle's dad got out of the car and went inside the gym. "It looks great inside. I'm glad to see plenty of teachers and volunteers. Michelle, there's a lot of food this year."

"Thanks for dropping us off, Dad. See you later." Michelle's dad hugged her and waved goodbye to us.

"Enjoy the dance and stay out of trouble, girls. Sydney, your mom will pick you guys up later, right?"

"Yes, my mom is coming by around ten o'clock. Thank you."

The assistant principal greeted us at the top of the stairs. She told us to stay near the entrance and don't venture to other areas of the school. The music blasted. Loads of swaying balloons hung from the ceiling, with strobe lights lighting up the dance floor.

Michelle pointed, laughing. "Look at that food table. It almost stretches across the whole gym."

A banner with bold black letters hung from the ceiling that read, "WE WILL NEVER FORGET YOU, DARYL!!!" It sure didn't mean much to me, but I neglected to even ask about it.

Michelle grabbed my hand and dragged me toward a group of girls dancing together. I heard my heart thumping. The girls nodded as we fell in step with the music.

"The music is great. You're a good dancer, Sydney." Michelle was a well-oiled machine on the dance floor, but not in a showing-off kind of way like some of the girls.

I shouted at Michelle. "I need to get hydrated. I'll be right back. I weaved my way over to the food table for a bottle of water. As I turned to look for Michelle, a guy sprinted over to ask her to dance, and before long, an assembly of guys huddled around her, dancing away.

Michelle waved at me. "Sydney, come over and dance with us." She kept waving me over, but I hesitated.

I looked around and hoped someone would ask me to dance, but nobody did. I ran into the bathroom. My palms were sweaty. I took a deep breath and went back out, putting on a smiling face and hoping things would get better.

Michelle spotted me and hurried over. "Where did you go? I've been looking all over for you. Are you all right?"

I shrugged. "I went to fix my hair."

"You look great. Your hairstyle is superb." Michelle was having such a good time. I didn't want to ruin it for her and kept my uneasiness to myself.

The guys never stopped hovering around Michelle. Negative thoughts spun through my head; I was convinced the guys disliked me.

I pretended to wave at someone on the opposite side of the dance floor. "I see a friend I want to talk to, Michelle."

"Do you want me to come along with you?" asked Michelle.

I forced a smile. "No, it's all right. I'll see you later." I wanted to get away and hide in a corner for a while.

Michelle high-fived me. "Look for me when you're finished talking with your friend. I'll be hanging around the dance floor somewhere or at the food table."

I lumbered away, making sure Michelle couldn't see the gloom on my face. "Yeah. I'll come to look for you later."

Chapter 7

As I stood in a corner alone, staring down at my shoes, a pair of feet appeared in my view. "Sorry to disturb you, but I've never seen you here before. I'm Shawn."

I raised my head, glancing up at him. I didn't recognize him from school but assumed our paths never crossed. "Hello," I mumbled, fidgeting with my hair.

Shawn extended his arm for a handshake. "I didn't catch your name. If you're waiting for someone and want me to go away, let me know."

I chuckled and shook his hand. "No, I'm not waiting for anyone. My name is Sydney. You caught me by surprise." I couldn't help but notice his facial hair, which I had never seen on any of the guys at school before.

Shawn hesitated and brought his hand to his chin. "Were you at the dance last year?"

"No, this is my first dance here. I've been at Winter Garden less than a year."

"Yeah. That's what I thought. I try to welcome the students coming to the dance for the first time. It's my job, and I'm pretty good at remembering faces. Where did you go to school before coming here?"

"I went to John Burroughs in Michigan. It's kind of far from here."

"Whoa! It sure is far from here," said Shawn. "I've been to Michigan before."

I talked about my moving experiences and the hard times I went through. "I always hope things would get better each time we moved. The first day at a new school was the worse."

Shawn nodded. "I remember those first days at school, having to introduce myself all the time, eating lunch alone, and having people stare at me as I walked through the hallway."

My mouth dropped open. "You moved a lot, too?"

"Uh-huh. My dad was in the military, and we moved all the time. He's retired from the military for two years now on a medical discharge."

"I know what you mean. Opening the classroom door on my first day and getting twenty eyeballs staring at you all at once sure didn't make me feel welcomed."

"Tell me about it," said Shawn.

"It was always embarrassing when the teacher asked me to stand up and introduce myself."

Shawn shook his head. "How about desperately running around trying to find your classroom before the bell rang? I still remember asking for directions to the bathrooms, only to get laughed at."

"Yeah. How about walking down the hallway and hearing students laughing and clowning around, just feeling like you were the only one in school who didn't know anyone?"

He nodded. "Exactly. Well, it looks like we have something in common at least."

I laughed. "We sure do."

"It's a little too noisy in here," said Shawn. "Do you want to go outside and maybe get something to drink? But only if you want to. I don't want us to lose our voices screaming over the music."

"Yeah. Let me tell my friend, Michelle. I'll be right back." I hunted all over the dance floor and finally spotted Michelle at the food table scrounging for food.

"Hey, Michelle," I hollered, flapping my arms over my head. She turned around and rambled over toward me, chomping on a slice of pizza.

She grinned. "Where were you? I'm going to get another slice of pizza before it's all gone. Come with me. You love pizza."

"Hey, I'm going outside with Shawn for a while. I just wanted to tell you."

Michelle scrunched her face, then laughed. "I know Shawn, and now you know Shawn, too. Great."

"I just met him. I'll talk to you later."

"Yup." Michelle strolled off and disappeared into the crowd.

I went to get my scarf before meeting up with Shawn. He stood by the door holding a tray with a couple of sodas and cake. His head stood above everyone else's. I took a deep breath and weaved my way through the traffic to where Shawn waited.

I tapped his shoulder. "I'm ready."

"Oh, there you are. Hey, I got a couple of drinks and cake, too."

"Yeah, I noticed. Are you sharing it with me?" I couldn't help teasing him. I felt comfortable hanging around with Shawn, knowing Michelle didn't seem to have a problem with it. He was polite and considerate, not something I got from most of the guys at school.

"Of course, it's for both of us," said Shawn. "By the way, I know Michelle."

"Oh, thank you. Can I help you hold something? Yeah, she's my best friend." We headed outside. The parking lot lights lit up the entire area around the gym. I could still hear the music— but less noisy for sure. Some students I knew waved at me as we walked by.

Shawn perused the area. "I don't see an empty table anywhere."

I held onto my scarf as the wind kicked up. "It's getting a little cold."

"I could give you my jacket," said Shawn, "Sorry. I mean, do you need to get your jacket?"

"No, I'm fine. Thank you." I looped my scarf around a few more times.

Shawn spun around. "Someone is leaving. Let's hurry and get that table. Wait a minute. I need to go back inside for napkins. Can you hold the table until I get back?"

"I got the napkins, and I have toothpicks, too."

He raised an eyebrow. "Are you always so prepared?"

I laughed. "That's what Michelle tells me all the time."

Chapter 8

"You got a pretty big slice of cake there."

Shawn scratched his head. "I guess I forgot to cut it into two pieces. Here's a plastic knife. Can you cut it, please? You're probably better at it than me."

I tucked my hair behind my ears and sliced away. "Whoops. I hope the pieces are about the same size."

He chuckled. "One piece looks a tiny bit bigger, but you can take the larger one."

"All right. Mmm, the cake is so good. You should try it."

Shawn shoved a piece into his mouth and continued to talk. "Yeah. It was hard moving all the time for me, too. My brother and I went to Winter Garden together at first. He had just started middle school." He coughed from the cake in his mouth.

I handed Shawn his soda. "How about you?"

"I entered as an eighth-grader. Thanks, I should know better not to talk with my mouth full."

"Funny, I've never seen you at school." I touched my cheek to let him know he had frosting on his face.

Shawn grabbed a napkin and dabbed it off. "Oh, thanks. I am in high school now—graduated last year."

I nodded. "Oh, yeah. You did say you were in the eighth grade when you moved here. Did you like going to Winter Garden with him?"

"I did." Shawn took another gulp of his soda. "My brother needed special tutoring after school to keep up in class. I didn't understand why the teacher thought he needed tutoring. His classmates called him the weird kid."

I shook my head. "Not nice. Just because someone is different doesn't make them weird."

Shawn shrugged. "His classmates picked on him all the time. The joking turned into bullying. I got upset when I found out."

"Awww, what a bunch of meanies. I'm lucky no one picked on me. My classmates just snubbed me most of the time. But I did feel insecure, worrying all the time about having to move again."

"The funny thing is, he listened to everything the pastor talked about at church—no fidgeting around like he did in class," said Shawn.

"Yeah. God's words can sure get our attention sometimes. It's good you go to church with your brother. My brother likes to stay home. We remind him about the free donuts to encourage him to go to church with us."

He leaned forward. "And get this, I would see him praying out loud as if Jesus was right there in his room with him. Sometimes, he would kneel next to his bed, and other times he just stood there, staring up at the ceiling with his arms over his head."

"I guess it made him feel safe and loved. I hope he still prays every day."

"Yeah. You're probably right," said Shawn, twitching around in his seat.

"That's what I do after an awful day at school. It stopped me from smashing things against the wall." I snickered. Something seemed weird when I asked Shawn about his brother. But I couldn't quite put my finger on why.

Shawn smiled. "Whenever I went to a new school, my mom told me to join a club right away. She worried about us whenever we moved."

"My grandma and I would have a long talk every time we moved. She helped me prepare, which got me through the first week or so of school."

"I'm kind of good at sports, so I joined the baseball team," said Shawn. "It helped me make friends pretty fast."

"Oh, so cool. I'm not good at sports."

He laughed. "You're probably better at sports than you think."

"I never thought about joining a club right away. I'm on the shy side. Sometimes it would be weeks and maybe longer before I found someone I could talk to."

"It must have been hard, Sydney."

"Yeah. I guess the bullying stopped."

Shawn sipped his soda and paused. "It did stop, but I hated those guys for doing that to him."

"More than one person bullied your brother? Terrible."

"Yeah. A whole group of guys who hung around together bullied him." He shook his head. "The leader of the group did most of the pushing and name-calling. It didn't bother Daryl much, but it sure bothered me."

"Your brother is an inspiration."

"Yeah. I looked up to my little brother. It had a lot to do with his faith and trust in God. He talked about God more than me. My parents wanted to send them to a special school to help him with his learning disability and also to protect him."

"Oh, I see. Your brother is away at school. I hope things are better for him there."

Shawn paused, staring out across the parking lot. "Sydney, my brother died about a year and a half ago."

I slumped down, putting my hands over my mouth. Shawn wiped the tears that trickled down his cheek. I reached for a napkin. I finally got why he talked about his brother the way he did.

"What happened?" I whispered. "Never mind, I shouldn't be asking. I'm sorry."

Shawn's voice cracked. "Yeah. It's kind of a long story and hard to talk about sometimes. It brings back too many bad memories. I don't think I'll ever get over it. I think about him every day." He turned away, covering his face.

I reached over and touched his shoulder. "Are you all right, Shawn? Maybe we should go back inside."

He ruffled his hair and took a deep breath. "I want to share with you what happened. It will be my way of honoring him today."

"Are you sure?"

He clenched his hands over his head. "After school, I walked behind my brother to keep an eye on him along with some friends of mine. I wanted to make sure no one would bother him anymore, especially those bullies in his class. He knew I was close by somewhere."

I nodded. "Good idea. You were a good brother to him. I know it, and your brother knew it too for sure."

Shawn took a breath. "The group of bullies walked in front of him, clowning around that day. And the guy who bullied my brother the most tripped and stumbled into the street. I saw a truck speeding toward him. My brother dropped his backpack and dashed over as fast as he could. It happened so fast. I shouted at my brother to get out of the street. He pushed the guy out of the way of the speeding truck."

"Your brother saved the bully."

"Yeah. But the truck hit my brother," said Shawn.

"Oh, no!" I buried my face in my hands.

Shawn fidgeted with his empty can of soda. "He flew into the air and landed on top of the hood of the truck. The paramedics rushed him to the hospital. He stayed in a coma for a month before he died. I prayed so hard for him—should have walked closer behind. I could have pulled him out of the way."

"It's not your fault. You know it's not, Shawn." I wanted to say something to help him feel better but couldn't find the words.

Shawn leaned back in his chair. "Everyone from school sent him cards, and even people who didn't know him came to see Daryl in the hospital. I miss him so much. He taught me more about God, kindness, and forgiveness than anyone. Winter Garden wanted to honor my brother, and that is why we have a dance for him every year."

I smiled. "I didn't know that." I finally got it. The name *Daryl* on the banner hanging from the ceiling was Shawn's brother.

"I have all the local newspaper articles about what happened," said Shawn. "I hated God for allowing this to happen and stopped praying and going to church for the longest time. I got angry a lot and even got into trouble at school, which isn't like me at all."

I tried not to interrupt him. Grandma always allowed me to talk about my problems. It helped me see situations differently and made me feel better.

Shawn hung his head. "He would tell me to pray for the bullies, but I just wanted to strangle them."

"He's an amazing person."

"Friends at church helped me get the revenge out of my system. I prayed all the time and finally forgave those guys. It took a long time." Shawn closed his eyes and tilted his head up toward the sky.

"I don't know if I would be able to forgive them. I'm even angry at those guys."

Shawn grinned. "Are you the oldest one?"

"Yeah. I have a little brother. I helped take care of my brother. Both my mom and dad worked, and I hardly saw my dad back then. I haven't quite forgiven him for making me change schools so much."

Shawn looked away for a second, tapping his finger on his chair. "Too bad. My relationship with my dad is great now. I realized the last thing he wanted to do was make things miserable for me. He sacrificed way more than I could imagine."

Chapter 9

Shawn glanced at his watch. "My dad is coming to pick me up soon. Maybe we should clean up our trash."

"Can you hand me a napkin to wipe off the table, please?"

Shawn grinned. "You're not only prepared all the time but tidy. I thought moms were the only ones interested in keeping everything clean and tidy. Maybe you're a Girl Scout."

"Nope. But I thought about joining. The trash bins are over there, Shawn. You know, I wish I had a chance to meet your brother."

He nodded. "Yeah. I never met anyone as faithful as Daryl. Things were just a lot harder for him, but he never let stuff get him down. I can't understand how people can be so mean."

I shook my head. "Middle-graders are so nasty to each other sometimes. I hope it's better in high school."

"In a way, it gets better," said Shawn. "You know, Daryl didn't quite get sports, but he cared for people. At church, Daryl would help the elderly and those in wheelchairs all the time. He had this radar to detect people who needed help. Do you know anyone like that?"

"Yeah. I do. My grandma cares a lot about people. She has a special radar just like Daryl."

"And she doesn't quite get sports either," said Shawn.

We both laughed.

Shawn got up and stretched, then sat back down. "Sometimes, I noticed things were bothering Daryl, and I tried to help him. But he ended up helping me; so weird. He could almost read my mind."

"My grandma has a way of putting things in perspective for me. She knows me inside and out and can almost read my mind, too."

Shawn nodded. "Hey, I like the word *perspective*. It makes you sound intelligent."

"Maybe you should start using the word. It never hurts to sound more intelligent." I covered my mouth to stifle a giggle. I heard someone tapping their car horn. "Is that your dad, Shawn?"

He stood up to get a better view. "Yeah. It's his car, all right. Sorry, I got to leave."

I smiled. "I'm glad I met you today. I had fun talking about everything. Maybe I'll see you around again one of these days." I made a new friend at the dance, but I honestly thought I would never talk to Shawn again for some silly reason.

"I had a good time, too," said Shawn. "I'll see you at church."

I shot him a double-take. "What do you mean?"

"We go to the same church. I remember seeing you there now. Is that your little brother?"

"I just started going there not too long ago. Yeah. That's my little brother. What a coincidence. Is this a God wink moment, Shawn?"

He held his finger up to ask his dad to wait a minute. "Not sure. Anyway, I'm part of the youth ministry. I'll look for you on Sunday."

"And I'll look for you, too."

"Okay, we have a deal. Let me walk back with you." Shawn stood at the bottom of the stairs and waited as I climbed the stairs to the gym doors.

"Bye, thank you. See you at church. Your dad is still waiting. Better hurry."

Shawn stuck his head out the car window as his dad pulled away. "Sydney, see you Sunday."

I stayed outside a little longer, thinking. I wondered if I loved God as much as Daryl. Jesus was his best friend, a friend he talked to about everything in his life. When Shawn told me he forgave his brother's bullies, it made me question if I needed to be more kind and forgiving. I thought about the grudge I held against Dad, too.

Two guys whispered to each other as they walked by me. "Why is she staring up at the sky?" I had a habit of looking up when I thought about things. Still upset about hearing what happened to Shawn's brother, I glared at them. It made me sad, seeing how much Daryl's passing away still hurt Shawn.

Grandma told me lots of times that God often sends us friends to help us. But at other times, He sends difficult people and situations into our lives to make us stronger. She understood what I had to go through as a new kid at school for sure.

Michelle peeked outside. "Sydney, I'm going to get some more food before it's all gone. Come with me. Did Shawn go home already?"

"He just left. His dad picked him up. Hey, I found out he goes to the same church as me. You go ahead, Michelle. I'm right behind you." The winds kicked up and tossed my hair all over the place. I never met anyone who thought about food as much as Michelle.

Car headlights bounced off the side of the gym as more cars pulled in and out of the parking lot. Half of the students had already gone home. Even though I got off to a rough start at the dance, getting a chance to share stories with Shawn about our mutual moving nightmares made it all worth it.

Chapter 10

I went inside to find Michelle. As I headed toward the food table, Katherine, from one of my classes, jumped in front of me, blocking my way. She squinted her eyes at me then jabbed her finger into my chest. "Why didn't you apologize? So rude of you."

I pushed her hand away. "What are you talking about?" I turned around and walked away, hoping she would stop bothering me.

Katherine continued to follow me. "Where do you think you're going? Don't try to pretend you didn't do it."

I glared at her. "I know I didn't do anything to you."

Katherine stuck her tongue out at me. "Look at my blouse. You ruined it." Her friends rolled their eyes and shouted at me. Students rushed over, bumping against each other as they formed a circle around us.

"It wasn't me. You're mixing me up with someone else. Leave me alone."

Katherine pumped her fist. "No, it was you. I'm not mixing you up with anyone." She was one of the noisy students in class, always bothering the students sitting around her. I had never talked to her before and had no idea why she disliked me so much.

She shoved me into the crowded of students standing behind me. Two girls grabbed my arms so I wouldn't fall. "What do you think you're doing? Stop it!"

Michelle pushed her way through the crowd. "Are you all right, Sydney?"

I took a deep breath. "I'm glad you're here."

Michelle sneered at Katherine, wagging her finger at her. "Why are you pushing her? You better stop causing trouble."

As I walked toward her to shove her back, a teacher rushed over to break up the commotion. Katherine stepped away and headed for the doors with her friends. She swung around and glared at me. "You haven't heard the end of this."

The teacher stared at the students who were still hovering around me. "I'm ready to sign up anyone interested in detention time after school. All right then. Let's break this party up."

I thought about explaining what happened to the teacher but decided it wouldn't make the situation better. The music cranked up again, and everyone went off in different directions.

Michelle grabbed my hand and dragged me over to the corner of the gym. "What just happened?"

"Katherine said I caused her to spill her drink on her blouse. I don't remember it happening. I can't believe someone would make something up and blame me for it. I'm confused."

Michelle huffed. "No way. I don't remember either. Don't pay her any attention. She's just a mean and jealous person."

I wrinkled my nose. "What do you mean by jealous person? I know you don't mean she's jealous of me."

"Well, I have a theory," said Michelle. "You and I know she is one of those mean girls in school. And, you know the guy who sits next to you in class, right?"

"Yeah. Katherine is always bothering people, and of course, I know the guy who sits next to me. He's nice, and we help each other with homework sometimes. But what does he have to do with this situation?"

Michelle nodded. "This means you guys are friends."

"Yeah. You can call us friends. What are you getting at? Stop beating around the bush, Michelle. Please, spit it out."

"All right, all right. I heard Katherine has a big crush on the guy. C'mon! You know what I mean. She considers you big competition."

"That's why she's so mean to me? You're kidding."

Michelle shook her head. "Nope. I'm not kidding. It's part of the rumor mill around here. But since Katherine wasn't bothering you, I figured she didn't like the guy anymore. I sure got it wrong."

"Yeah. You're right about that. Michelle, you should've told me anyway. Thanks for warning me, pal."

She gave me a half-smile. "I'm sorry. The guy doesn't even like her."

"So here I am, minding my own business, and this happens. Don't worry about it. It's not your fault. But now that I know, I'll be more careful."

"Hey, your eyes are closed. Don't tell me you're praying again. Yeah. It's best to be more careful when Katherine's around."

"Yes, I'm praying. I'm asking God to help me forgive her and to let this be the end of it." I tried not to let it bother me. But Katherine's parting words didn't give me confidence we wouldn't bump heads again.

Michelle smiled. "You're practically a saint. I would never forgive her."

"Hahaha. If you hear something, please let me know right away this time."

Michelle nodded. "Yeah, right away. I got your back, and I'll keep my eyes and ears open."

"I hope this doesn't turn into a big problem, and I don't want to be part of the gossip at school, either."

Michelle wrapped her arm around my arm. "Don't worry. I won't let anything happen to you. That's what best friends do. Just call me mama bear."

I laughed. "Yes, mama bear. You're the best." Having Michelle around sure made the situation less scary.

She glanced over at the food table. "I hope there's still food left. Want me to get you something?"

I grinned, shaking my head. "No, I'm not hungry anymore."

Chapter 11

Our assistant principal stopped the music and turned off some of the lights. "Thank you for attending the dance," he announced. "Please gather up your possessions. We will be locking the gym doors soon."

The volunteers and teachers herded us out. I waited at the bottom of the stairs for Mom to pick us up. It got pretty noisy outside, and with dark and gray rain clouds gathering in the distance, it looked like we might get rain.

"I kind of regret coming to the dance. Katherine ruined everything for me."

Michelle frowned. "I'm sorry it happened. And I'm sorry for not spending more time with you. I got a little too distracted."

"It's not your fault. My intuitions told me something awful might happen at the dance, and it did."

Michelle stared at me. "Wait a second. Does this mean you didn't have fun hanging around with Shawn?"

I smiled. "You're right. I did have a good time hanging around with Shawn. With all the drama, I forgot about the new friend I made. Thanks for reminding me, and sorry for being such a gloomy friend. Why didn't you ever tell me about Shawn and his brother, Daryl?"

She looked away for a second. "I hate to admit it, but I stopped thinking about why we have this dance, which is to honor the memory of Daryl, of course."

"It's my fault. My first-dance worries got the best of me. I didn't even bother to ask you what the banner staring me in the face, with Daryl's name on it, meant."

"Yeah. So, what did you guys talk about?" asked Michelle. "You two were outside for a while."

"Well, Shawn told me about the story behind the dance, which my best friend forgot to mention anything to me about."

I laughed.

She gave me a stern look and huffed. I buttoned my coat up to the top and tugged the scarf around my neck as the winds kicked up.

Michelle's face softened. "Yeah. Daryl always sat by himself at lunch and seemed shy. Some of the guys gave him a hard time in class. He brought his Bible to school."

"He did? I've never seen anyone with a Bible at school. What a faithful Christian."

Michelle nodded. "I even saw him reading it and praying at lunch. A lot of the guys made fun of him, but he never got mad."

"Shawn did mention Daryl loved God. It's funny. I can relate to Daryl's problems at school but in a different way. His story touched me deep inside."

"I'm sure being unconventional made it harder for Daryl to make friends," said Michelle.

"I'm upset people would pick on someone just because they're not like them. It's not right we have to try to be like everyone else to be accepted."

Michelle dipped her head. "Some of the guys felt bad about bullying him, especially after what happened. They even went to see him in the hospital. Daryl is a hero. It's unbelievable what he did."

"Yeah. That's what I heard from Shawn. He got choked up, and he choked me up, too. I didn't even know Daryl, but what I heard about him today changed me."

"You guys had a serious talk. Hey, is that your mom's car?" Michelle pointed to the back of the parking lot.

"Yeah, it's her all right. I don't know anyone else with a green station wagon. Let's get going. You have all your things?"

"Wait. I forgot to get my jacket."

Mom spotted me and stuck her head out the car window. She tapped the horn. "Sydney, I'm over here."

"Wait a minute, Mom," I shouted. "Michelle is inside looking for her jacket."

She finally ran out. "I found it. I took longer than I thought— spooky inside with only a couple of lights on."

I slumped into the back seat. "Hi, Mom. Do you know you have a pot of flowers back here?"

Michelle smiled. "Thank you for driving me back home."

"You're welcome. Darling, thanks for reminding me. I bought them today and forgot to take them out of the car."

I pushed the flowers over to the side to make room for Michelle to sit. You could always find gardening supplies in the back seat of Mom's car.

As Mom drove toward Michelle's house, she glanced back at us through the rear-view mirror. "You guys are pretty quiet back there. Did you two have a good time at the dance?"

Michelle and I glanced and each other, grinning. I didn't want to go into what happened at the dance yet. "It went pretty good, Mom. I made a new friend. I found out he goes to our church.

We'll see him on Sunday." Katherine's last words were still fresh in my head. I wondered what she had up her sleeve.

Once Michelle arrived home, she grabbed her jacket and nodded at me as she climbed out of Mom's car. "Bye, thank you again for driving me back. See you later, Sydney. We need to talk."

Mom glanced back at me. "Hey, what does that mean? It sounds serious. She honked, and the porch light came on.

Michelle's mom popped open the front door, waving at us. "Thank you. I might come by next week to see how your garden is doing and have a cup of coffee."

"Drop by whenever you have time. You know where to find me," said Mom. "You can help me pick some fresh tomatoes."

"Sure. So long as you give me a few to take home for dinner." Michelle's mom laughed and waved goodbye.

Chapter 12

I had finally stopped worrying about moving all time, and life at Winter Garden Middle School looked great with plenty of good days in store. But with Katherine making me a target of her anger, my cheery little world changed.

Mom stuck her head out the window and backed her car into the driveway. "Please help me put the pot of flowers in the backyard. Don't get your dress dirty, darling." She fumbled around for the light switch in the patio.

I grabbed the flower from the backseat, making sure not to get anything on my clothes. "I'll put the flowers by the back door. Mom, it's really cold out here."

She rushed over to unlock the back door. "Perfect! Let's get inside before we freeze. It looks like rain is coming. How about something warm to drink?"

I nodded. "What about having hot cocoa with marshmallows on top?"

Mom smiled. "Love the idea, darling. Yeah. It will take only a second to make the hot cocoa. I have a few marshmallows left over from Christmas somewhere. Hey, I found them."

"Check the expiration date, Mom. I've never seen a marshmallow that color before."

"No expiration date. But marshmallows keep for a long time.

So, how did your first dance go?" Mom asked again as she poured the hot cocoa.

I passed on the marshmallows. I warmed my hands with my cup of cocoa and blabbed to Mom what happened at the dance.

Mom grinned. "I knew I could get to the bottom of why you guys were so quiet in the car. You can't fool your mother."

I groaned. "I hope this is the end of it."

Mom gazed into my eyes, huffing. "I going to talk to someone at school to make sure this girl doesn't try anything else."

I smiled. "No worries. I'll let you know if I need your help. Can I talk to Grandma? I promised to tell her how the dance went as soon as I got home. Grandma looked worried when I told her I was stressing out about the dance."

"You make sure to let me know if this girl continues to bother you," said Mom. "I know you had a bit of a hard time at the dance and want to tell Grandma all about it, but I need to tell you what happened when you were away."

"Tell me what?"

Mom ran her hands through her hair and paused. "Grandma is sick, and we need to take her to the hospital to get some tests."

"What's wrong with Grandma? She didn't seem sick when she left to go shopping with her friends."

Mom grabbed my hand. "When she came home, Grandma didn't feel well, and it got worse."

"She's going to be fine, right?" I wanted so badly to talk with Grandma after the dance. If anyone could get me through this problem with Katherine, she would know how to do it. But Grandma's condition was way more important than anything else.

"We'll find out more after we see the doctor. It's kind of late, and she needs rest. Besides, you need to get some rest too."

From the quiver in Mom's voice, I knew Grandma had something more than a cold. As I trotted upstairs, I stopped at Grandma's room and peeked inside. Grandma rolled her head from side to side once in a while and mumbled as she slept. Her face looked pale. I had never seen her so sick before. My brother's bedroom door swung open, and he rushed over. "Sydney, did you hear about Grandma? She's sick. I heard Mom talking to the doctor."

"Yeah. Mom told me when I got back from the school dance."

My brother took a deep breath. "She sure is sleeping a lot. I hope Grandma gets better soon."

"Let's go to my room and pray for her." We knelt beside the bed like we once did as little kids. I closed my eyes and pushed some tears away. *"God, please guide the doctors to make Grandma well again. We need your help to heal her. We love her so much and don't want anything to happen to her. Amen."*

"I'm going back to my room, Sydney. Nothing bad is going to happen to Grandma, right?" My brother forced a worried smile as he stepped out of the room.

I closed my eyes and prayed some more. Then, I heard Grandma moaning and hurried back to her room. Mom glanced at me, holding a spoon. "She's not eating anything."

"Let me help, Mom. I can do it." Grandma always took good care of me. I wanted so much to help her in any way I could.

Mom nodded. "All right. You can see if you can get Grandma to eat her soup. I'm not having much luck." Mom tucked another napkin under Grandma's chin and handed me the bowl of chicken soup, making sure not to drip it on me.

I scooted closer to her and whispered, "Grandma, it's me, Sydney. Please have some of your soup. It will make you feel better." She squinted at me and cracked open her mouth. I touched the spoon to her lower lip, and she sipped. "Yes, she's eating." Grandma finished half of her soup and fell back asleep.

Mom smiled. "You had more luck feeding her than me. I think this is the best we can do, darling. She's not going to eat anymore."

Mom removed the cushions that propped Grandma up to eat and lowered her head onto the pillow. I grabbed the washcloth on the tray and dabbed Grandma's mouth. "Sydney, please take the tray down for me. I want to watch her for a while."

"I can stay with her for you."

Mom nodded. "All right. If Grandma looks like she's uncomfortable, make sure to get me right away."

"Will do."

I sat on the edge of the bed and gazed at Grandma as she slept. Her breathing broke the silence in the room. I tried not to make any noise. But after a while, I got this urge to talk to her.

I whispered into her ear. "Grandma, I had a good time at the dance, except for one problem. I almost got in a fight with a girl from one of my classes. She lied about everything in front of everyone at the dance. I hoped no one believed her. Even though this awful situation happened, I still had a good time and made a new friend, too. He goes to our church."

I could almost hear her talking back to me—asking me to pray more and allowing time for God to tell me what to do next.

Mom stomped up the stairs to look in on me. "Is everything fine with Grandma?"

"She's good. We had a nice talk. Grandma didn't say anything, but I heard her loud and clear."

"Oh, that's great," said Mom. "You got to talk to her, after all."

"I'm going back to my room now. I'm a little tired."

Mom smiled. "Thank you for all your help, darling. Get some rest. You had a long day."

"Bye, Grandma. I'll talk to you soon." I wanted to hug Grandma, but I gently squeezed her hand instead and tip-toed out of the room.

As I lay on my bed staring at the ceiling, I reminisced about all the fun times Grandma and I shared. Curling up under the covers, I prayed one more time for her to get better.

Chapter 13

Dad pulled up behind a line of cars in front of the school and dropped me off. My parents changed their work schedule to make sure someone stayed with Grandma. I was having a hard time keeping my mind off her.

Standing under the oak tree waiting for me as usual, Michelle waved me down. "Hey, did you get all your homework done? I did somehow. But going to the movies with my parents didn't help. I loved the movie, though."

"Yeah. I finished my homework, but my grandma is sick. I prayed for her all weekend. I found out when I got home from the dance after dropping you off."

Michelle slipped on her backpack. "You do look a little tired. Let's get going. I want to unload some books before class."

"Yeah, I didn't sleep too well. Can you help please pray for my grandma? She needs all the prayers she can get." Mom talked to the pastor and friends at church over the weekend to pray for Grandma, too.

Michelle grinned. "But, I'm not a Christian."

"You can still help pray for my grandma. Just ask Jesus for His assistance. God will hear you."

Michelle nodded. "I'll do it for you and your grandma. I hope everything turns out all right. I know how close you're to her."

I stopped and turned away, tears filling my eyes. Michelle put her arm around my shoulder. "I'm sorry. We'd better hurry up."

"Thank you for praying for her. I'm so worried. By the way, I'm waiting for your answer about coming to church with me."

Michelle shrugged. "I'll let you know when I'm ready."

"You know what it's like to wait for someone to make a decision. I'm just giving you a gentle reminder."

"Yeah, it's like me having to wait for your decision about the dance, Sydney."

I smiled. "Exactly."

* * *

Mrs. Clark looked around the classroom. "Please, pass your homework forward. Let's hurry up. We have plenty to cover this morning."

I searched through my backpack and finally found my homework buried between the pages of a book, which had never happened before.

"Before we get started, I have an announcement to make." From Mrs. Clark's stern expression, I knew it wouldn't be one of her regular morning announcements. "As you may know, there's been excess talking in class the last few weeks. It bothers me, and I'm sure it's bothering many of you. So, I decided to make seating changes to address the problem."

The students whined and jawed about it with their neighbors. I didn't talk a lot in class, so I figured she wouldn't move my seat.

Mrs. Clark put her hand up to quiet the class. "Sorry, this is the best solution for now." First, she called out the names of the noisy students to move, but she also called on students I considered the quiet ones in class.

Michelle turned around and shrugged her shoulders at me. My palms got clammy as she called on a few more of the quiet students. I liked where I sat and the classmates around me.

Mrs. Clark scanned the classroom, verifying her list of seating changes. "Sydney, you'll move to the desk in front of Katherine."

I tossed my arms in the air and almost fell off my chair. Of all the students Mrs. Clark could've picked for me to sit next to, she decided to put me right in front of my least favorite person in the world.

Mrs. Clark nodded. "If the noise in class continues, I'll make more seating changes. Please, gather your possessions if I called your name and go to your new desk. Keep the noise down. Thank you for cooperating."

I threw my backpack over my shoulder and grabbed my book. Katherine glared at me, chuckling as I walked toward her. Brushing a strand of hair from my face, I sneered and turned up my nose at her.

"Please, let's hurry up," said Mrs. Clark. "I still have a class to teach. I need to cover the material you'll need for your homework assignment."

Shaking my head, I slumped into my chair and unpacked. I glanced at Michelle across the room as she cupped her mouth with her hand. She made a face that said it all. Katherine tapped me on the shoulder and whispered, "I guess you're not sitting by your boyfriend anymore."

I snapped back. "A friend, not a boyfriend. You got it?"

"Sydney, please turn around in your seat," said Mrs. Clark. "Are you rolling eyes at someone in particular?"

I wrinkled my nose. "Sorry, Mrs. Clark. But Katherine is

bothering me. Never mind."

I couldn't wait another second for the class to end. The bell rang, and the students dashed out. "See you tomorrow, neighbor," said Katherine, chuckling again as she headed out the door.

Michelle stopped by my desk. "Sydney, I need to pick something up from my locker first. I'll wait for you outside afterward."

I gathered up my things and looked up at Mrs. Clark. I was upset and wanted her to know about it. Mrs. Clark raised an eyebrow as I walked past her. I saw Michelle probing through her locker and snuck up behind her. "Michelle, pinch me. Tell me it's a bad dream. I want to go somewhere and scream."

Michelle shook her head. "Sorry, it's not a dream. I don't know what to say." This situation was almost worse than moving to a new school. At least, no one ever hassled me there.

*   *   *

Katherine got more annoying as the weeks passed, not only in class but everywhere. She enjoyed drowning everyone out around her when she talked, interrupting people all the time. Katherine even tried to get my friends to stay away from me by bugging them to death.

Michelle and I sat at our usual place for lunch with friends, talking and laughing. Katherine wandered over to our table with her annoying friends. "Hey, does Sydney ever have anything interesting to say?"

Michelle stood up. "Shut your mouth. No one invited you to our table. Why don't you disappear—like right now."

Katherine chuckled. She strolled away, giving me one last

nasty sneer. I was looking over my shoulder all the time. She liked to sneak up on me and whisper insults to get under my skin.

"I had enough of Katherine. I need to do something about this."

Michelle nodded. "What do you have in mind?"

"I don't know yet." After school, I hurried over to Mrs. Clark's room to see if I could talk to her. I stood by the door, waiting for Mrs. Clark to notice me. But she continued to gather up the books lying around in her classroom. I cleared my throat.

Mrs. Clark swung around. "Oh, I didn't notice you standing there, Sydney. Can I help you with something?"

I pleaded. "Mrs. Clark, please change my seat. It's loud where I sit." I didn't dare to tell her the real reason.

Mrs. Clark grinned. "Sydney, I changed your seat because the loud students are getting too loud. It's the best I can do for now. Let's give it more time."

"If it doesn't get better, will you change my seat?" I whined and pleaded over and over.

Mrs. Clark smiled. "I hear you, Sydney. Thank you. I will consider your request. I have to go to a meeting. See you tomorrow."

Michelle waited for me in the hallway. "It looks like it didn't go so well. What did you tell her?"

I looked down. "I told Mrs. Clark the noise bothered me, and I wanted to change to another desk."

Michelle stared. "Why didn't you tell her the truth? She can't help you if you don't tell her the truth."

"Yeah. But I didn't. I'm afraid Katherine might find out I snitched on her, which will make my situation a lot worse. I need to figure out what to do. I'm going to go home and pray about it."

Michelle nodded. "I'm all ears. I don't want to see you upset all the time. It makes me feel miserable, too."

"Yeah, I'm sorry, Michelle. I might call you later."

Chapter 14

I prayed about what I should do next. In my heart, I knew the problem with Katherine wouldn't go away by itself. I got good grades, but concentrating during class got hard as she stepped up the harassment. I plopped down at my desk to do homework.

Mom marched in to see if I needed anything. "Hi darling, how's everything going?"

"Hi, Mom," I grumbled. I'd had some bad days where I would blow up at Mom for no reason. She sure didn't deserve any of it.

She raised an eyebrow. "Why so testy, darling? I hope you're not getting too much homework nowadays. I'll call you when dinner is ready." Mom gave me a quick squeeze and dashed out of the room.

I punched in Michelle's number. Her phone rang, then a second and third ring. "Thanks for picking up. Do you have time to talk? Sorry, I need to unload on you again."

"Just finished helping my mom in the kitchen," said Michelle. "I'm all ears."

"My situation with Katherine is getting worse. She never lets up. Some days it's about how terrible my hair looks. Other days, it might be something about my shoes or clothes. I can't take it any longer."

"I don't want to sound like a nag. But like I said, you need to let someone know. Stop hiding, Sydney."

"I can't get Katherine's sinister laugh out of my head. Even when I try to brush her off, she always finds a way to punch me in the gut. I have no idea how to get back at her. Whenever I tried, she finds another way to hurt me."

"Yeah, she can get pretty annoying," said Michelle. "I hate the way she rolls her eyes and throws her hair back all the time. She has a talent for hitting where it hurts—if you want to call it a talent."

"I'm kind of embarrassed to tell anyone, but I need help for sure. Maybe I should tell Mrs. Clark the real reason why I want to change seats."

"Now you're talking. Mrs. Clark did tell the class she's trained to help students with their problems at school, including problems with harassment and bullying. My mom is calling me for dinner. Sorry, I got to hang up. See you tomorrow."

I paced back and forth in my room like a caged animal, trying to pump myself up to tell Mrs. Clark. *Nothing is stopping me. I'm going to march into Mrs. Clark's room tomorrow morning and tell her everything. I'm not hiding it anymore.*

The decision to tell Mrs. Clark eased my worries, and I headed downstairs. "I can smell the casserole from upstairs, Mom. It's making me hungry."

Mom laughed. "Thanks for coming down, darling. Please, help me set the table. Dinner will be ready soon."

"Mom, can you drive me to school a little bit earlier tomorrow? Michelle and I are working on something we want to discuss with Mrs. Clark." With Grandma being sick and all, I didn't have the heart to tell Mom the real reason. Giving her more to worry about was the last thing I wanted to do.

Mom nodded. "How about ten to fifteen minutes earlier? Make sure you're ready."

"Perfect. Thank you, Mom."

* * *

I knocked on Mrs. Clark's classroom door. She scribbled something down in her notepad and glanced up at me. "Good morning, Sydney. What are you doing here so early?"

I wiped my sweaty palm against my jeans and took a big breath. "Uh, Mrs. Clark, I need to talk to you."

She walked over to the whiteboard. "Can it wait? I need to get ready for class."

"I'm getting bullied at school," I shouted.

Mrs. Clark turned around wide-eyed. "Please, come sit down. We hope you're all right. How long has this been going on?"

I frowned. "Well, at the dance, this girl said I caused her to spill something on her blouse. She lied about this for some reason, and we shouted at each other and almost got into a fight. Now she's bothering me all the time."

"I'm so sorry. You should've told me earlier."

"I figured it would go away by itself, but it didn't. Mrs. Clark, I'm stressed out."

Mrs. Clark huffed. "This has to stop. I'm glad you decided to come to talk to me. Sydney, bullying is always wrong. We can't have this at our school." Mrs. Clark made it loud and clear she wasn't going to put up with this.

I fidgeted with my hair. "What should I do? I'm afraid of what might happen when she finds out I talked to you."

"Sydney, we have been trained to handle these types of

situations with sensitivity, making sure not to put anyone into an even worse predicament. You did the right thing in letting me know. Students need to start following the rules around here. You need to tell me the name of this student."

I rested my head on my hand and stared out the window. *Shawn's brother forgave the boys that bullied him, and he had it a lot worse. At least, I needed to try to forgive her for what she did.*

Mrs. Clark shot back a concerned look. "Sydney, is something wrong? The student's name, please."

"Mrs. Clark, thank you for your time. The harassment isn't so bad—just a bunch of mean words."

She leaned forward, "Are you sure? We want to make sure you're safe. If your situation gets worse, don't wait to come to talk to me. All right, you know where to find me if you need help."

"Yeah. I'm sure, thank you for listening to my problem. I won't forget if it gets worse."

"Please close the door behind you," said Mrs. Clark. "Remember what we discussed today, Sydney."

I saw Michelle poking her head out from around the corner. "Hey, I see you. What are you doing here?"

She strolled over with her headsets on, humming to a song. "So, you told her about Katherine, right?" screamed Michelle.

I pointed at her headsets. "You're shouting at me. Take your headsets off. I changed my mind at the last minute. Something told me deep inside I needed to give Katherine a second chance."

Michelle threw her arms in the air. "You did what? Okay, let see how this turns out. I can't believe you walked out without saying a thing."

"I did tell Mrs. Clark what happened, but I didn't tell her it was Katherine. I know what I'm doing, and God will help me."

Michelle shook her head. "Wow! Mrs. Clark doesn't realize she moved you right in front of the girl who is now your worst nightmare. That's incredible."

"Yeah, if you want to put it that way." What a relief to know Mrs. Clark had my back. She cared about the students at Winter Garden Middle School and me personally, too.

Chapter 15

"Hey, I'm getting the news out around school about what Katherine is doing to you," said Michelle. "It's my battle against people like her. I want everyone at school to put pressure on Katherine to stop."

I smiled. "Yeah. I heard. You know, students I don't even know are encouraging me to hang in there. I appreciate what you're doing, Michelle. I don't know what to say." With the news out around school, Katherine's friends snubbed her, and even her crush told her to leave me alone. She got the hint and stopped harassing me.

I elbowed Michelle. "Look, Katherine is sitting by herself again. It reminds me of my days as a new student in school—a sad time I'd rather forget."

Michelle shook her head. "This is what she gets for lying and pushing my best friend around. Don't feel bad for her."

"Let's hurry up and finish our lunch. I need to make a stop at my locker to pick up a book for class."

Michelle nodded. "All right. I'll see you in class."

I grabbed the book I needed and made a mad dash. As I pushed through the classroom door, I dropped my backpack and books. Papers and pencils flew out all over the floor. Mrs. Clark shook her head. "Could someone help Sydney pick up her things?"

Katherine raised her hand right away. "I'll help." She picked up my books and even reached under Mrs. Clark's desk to grab the pencils that rolled underneath.

I turned around in my seat and looked at Katherine. "Thanks for helping me pick up my stuff." I braced for something mean to gush out her mouth.

Katherine whispered back. "You're welcome, and thank you for not snitching on me to Mrs. Clark."

"Sydney, it looks like you got all your things gathered up," said Mrs. Clark. "Katherine, thank you for helping." I saw Michelle busy passing out books to the class. She glanced over at me and shrugged her shoulders.

"No problems." Katherine smiled, dusting off her jeans.

Mrs. Clark tapped on the whiteboard. "May I have your attention, please? I know the due date for the science project seems like a ways off, but I suggest you get started sooner rather than later. And let me know who's in your science project group this week."

Katherine tapped me on the shoulder and whispered, "Hey, do you want to work on the science assignment together?"

"Uh, I'll talk to Michelle." I sure didn't expect this from Katherine. *Another one of God's challenges to me again,* I thought.

When the bell rang, Mrs. Clark called me over to her desk. "I know the name of the girl, Sydney. I hope your situation is better now. Again, let me know if it's not." I guessed she got wind of the news around school about Katherine.

As we headed to our lockers, Michelle nudged me. "Do you have any ideas for our science project? I'm sure you have a few thoughts on what you want to do. By the way, did Katherine give you a smart-aleck remark about dropping your backpack?"

"No, she didn't. Yeah. I do have a few ideas. We should talk about them. Maybe we can add someone to our science group."

Michelle nodded. "Awesome! I'm all for less work. Besides, it might be fun. I like how you're thinking ahead. Tell me more after school. Better yet, I'll call you tonight. You probably have someone in mind."

I smiled. "Yeah. I'll let you know when we talk tonight." I wanted to get my thoughts together before I broke the news that Katherine asked if she could join our science group.

Michelle waited for me as I fumbled around in my locker, which needed some spring cleaning for sure.

"Sydney, let me know, all right?" shouted Katherine, rushing to her next class.

"What does Katherine want you to tell her about?" asked Michelle, staring at me. "You know, I'm pretty curious now, so don't make me wait, Sydney. We need to talk at lunchtime."

I threw my head back, trying not to laugh. "Since you insist. Bye, see you then." I still had these not-so-good feelings toward Katherine, and something in me wanted a bit of revenge. But I knew God expected better from me.

*   *   *

The lunch bell finally rang, and everyone flew out of the classroom and headed to the lunch area. I dashed down the hall, crammed my backpack into my locker, and waited for Michelle to show up. Grandma usually packed lunch for me, but since she has been sick, Mom asked me to buy lunch at school instead.

Michelle raced around the corner. "Let's hurry before the line gets too long." Our fast walk turned into a dash to the finish line.

I nudged Michelle. "The line doesn't look too bad. I wish our school would give us more time for lunch. It looks like someone took our table already."

Michelle nodded. "We should try to make our lunches next time. It'll save time. We'll get our table back before you know it."

"Hey, I want to get something healthy to eat." Grandma trained me over the years to make healthy food choices.

Michelle scoped out the food options. "Let's get a slice of pie, a slice of pizza, and a fruit bowl. Fruit is healthy."

I laughed. "Sounds like an idea—something healthy, something tasty, and something delicious."

Michelle pointed at an empty table. "Hurry, get the spot over there, Sydney. I'm going to get some water."

I raced over and plunked my tray down to claim the table.

"I got you water, too," said Michelle. "So, what did Katherine want you to tell her?"

"It's about the science project." I didn't want to force Michelle to accept Katherine into our science group. But I wanted her to join.

Michelle avoided the fruit bowl and dove into her slice of pie. "Does she want to steal some project ideas from you? Mmm, the pie is so good."

"No. Katherine asked if she could join our science project group."

Michelle froze with her fork in her mouth for a second, with eyes popped wide open. "Why would I want her to join?"

"Katherine has changed, and I want to give her another chance. My grandma always told me everyone deserved a second chance."

Michelle grinned. "It looks like you've changed, too. Well, if it doesn't work out, we can always kick her out. And you and I can finish the project ourselves."

I nodded. "Besides, Katherine is pretty smart."

"Yeah. I remember Mrs. Clark giving us a hard problem to solve in class, and everyone got it wrong—except for Katherine. I couldn't believe it."

"All right. I'll let Katherine know she can join our group." I glanced over at her sitting alone at lunch again. I just knew God and Grandma would approve of my decision.

Michelle scratched her head. "Yeah. But if it doesn't work out, don't say I never told you so. Katherine isn't one of my top picks."

I laughed. "It's going to be fine. No worries."

Michelle peeked over at my piece of pie, which I hadn't touched yet. "Do you need help with your pie? I finished my slice already."

"Yeah. I noticed. What about your fruit bowl? It looks like you're not interested in fruit today."

"Since you already finished your fruit bowl, you can have my fruit bowl in exchange for some of your pie. You did say you wanted to eat healthy today."

I smiled. "It's a deal. You can have the whole slice." Michelle laughed and dug right in.

Chapter 16

Dad stood outside his car in the school parking lot. I had expected Michelle's mom to take us home after school. "That's weird. Why is my dad here to pick me up today?"

Michelle grinned. "Yeah, I see him waving at us. We should wave back to let him know we see him."

I threw my arms up in the air, signaling to Dad, then grabbed my backpack and moseyed over to him. Before I jumped into Dad's car, I shouted back at Michelle. "Please tell your mom I went home with my dad. I might call you tonight about the homework."

Michelle shot me a thumbs-up. "Will do. Talk to you later."

"You're normally at work, Dad. What's up?" I looked back and saw Michelle getting into her mom's car.

Dad hesitated and heaved a sigh. "I picked up a burger and some fries for you." He made a right at the corner and headed for the freeway entrance.

I looked at him. "Aren't we going home?"

"We need to see your grandma, darling. She's in the hospital and might need a medical procedure. But I'm not sure if it took place or not."

"What happened to her?" I stared at Dad, worrying about what he might say next. I closed my eyes and prayed for her.

"Your mom called me at work and told me she rushed Grandma to the hospital. I haven't heard from your mom in a while. We'll find out when we get there."

Mom never explained to me exactly what the doctor told her about Grandma's condition, but I was kind of afraid to ask. When we arrived at the hospital, the nurse told us Grandma needed a surgical procedure. "She should be out of surgery soon. The waiting room is down the hall to your left."

Dad led me down a hazily lit hallway. He stopped a nurse to confirm we didn't pass the room then increased his pace. "We're going in the right direction. Here's the room, Sydney."

I poked my head inside and saw Mom sitting in the corner with her head down. I rushed over to her. "Is Grandma going to be all right—and are you all right, too?"

Mom brushed her hair back, her eyes red and puffy. "Grandma should be coming out of surgery pretty soon. That's what the nurse last told me, but it's been a while."

"Good news, right?" I asked, draping my arms around Mom's shoulders.

A nurse knocked on the door and approached us. "The doctor would like to talk to you now. Please meet him in Conference Room 3 to your left."

"Please grab your mom's purse." Dad held Mom's hand and led her out.

As we entered the conference room, the doctor finished jotting something down and greeted us. "Please, have a seat." He gestured for us to take the chairs across from him.

Mom nervously rubbed her hands together. "Is she out of surgery, doctor?"

"Yes. But unfortunately, your mother suffered a heart attack.

We need to monitor her closely. She needs plenty of rest. Sorry, we can't allow you to visit her yet. But the good news is she's stable now."

Mom buried her face in her hands, whimpering. Dad tried to console her. My heart sank. I just stared at the doctor. He recommended moving Grandma to a nursing home to recover after she left the hospital.

I heard some noise outside the room. The nurses were wheeling Grandma into the ICU room. I pleaded to the doctor and Mom. "Please, let me see Grandma."

Mom grabbed some tissue to wipe my tears. "I'm so sorry, darling. Grandma is not well enough and needs a lot of rest. We have to wait until she's better."

Mom asked Dad to take me home and told him she would call when more information became available on Grandma's condition. I hugged Mom, whispering into her ear. "I want to stay with you. I can do my homework while we're waiting."

She glanced up at me, holding my hand. "I would love you to stay with me, but you should go home with your dad. I don't know long it might take, darling."

"Bye, Mom. Don't forget to call when you hear something."

"All right, darling. Love you."

Dad signed out, and we headed out the double front doors to the hospital parking lot. The sun had already set. "Dad, please tell me Grandma is going to be all right."

Dad forced a smile. "They're taking good care of Grandma. By the way, we need to make a stop to pick your brother up. He's at a friend's house. I'm going to order pizza for dinner."

I grinned. "All right, Dad."

Mom didn't come home that night from the hospital. Our

house was not the same without Grandma downstairs talking, laughing, cooking—taking care of us with so much love and happiness. I had so much I wanted to share with her. After finishing my homework, I prayed for the doctor and nurses to give Grandma the best care. I sure didn't want anything else to happen to her.

Chapter 17

After Grandma got better, Mom took me to visit her on Saturday mornings. I hadn't seen her in over two weeks. She signed in at the front desk and led me down a long hallway. "Grandma got moved to a new room last week."

"Mom, it's pretty crowded today." People in gowns sat around in wheelchairs outside their rooms, talking to their neighbors about the good old days. But a lot of patients sat all alone, too.

Mom nodded. "Yeah, family and friends usually come to visit on Saturdays and Sundays."

The nursing home had this odor I could never quite get used to even though I've been there a few times. Grandma shared her room with another lady. Mom kissed Grandma on the cheek and drew the curtain to give us more privacy.

I smiled. "Hi, Grandma. I missed you so much." I wanted to hug her, but the tubes and monitoring device attached to her caused me to hesitate.

Grandma snickered and reached out to hold my hand. "Get a chair and come sit next to me, darling. How's everything at school?"

I grabbed one of the chairs along the wall and dragged it next to her bed. "Things are going good with me. When are you coming home? I have so much I want to tell you."

Grandma shook her head. "I have no idea, darling. Ask your mom. Before I forget to ask, did you and Michelle have fun at the dance? I don't believe I got a chance to talk to you about it."

"Michelle and I had a fun time. I made a new friend. His name is Shawn. The dance went better than I thought, Grandma. Thank you for your advice and all your prayers. It helped for sure."

Grandma grinned with eyes half-closed. "I'm happy to hear everything went fine. Praise the Lord! I was a little worried about my sweet darling." Mom moved the bedside table closer to Grandma and tried to get her to eat her breakfast. As much as I wanted to tell her about everything that happened, I figured it would be better to focus on the positives and not mention anything about the skirmish I got into with Katherine.

"Mom, Grandma fell asleep again." We stayed all morning with Grandma. She slept most of the time.

Her nurse came into the room and checked the tube attached to her arm. "How are you today, ladies? It's time for your grandma to receive her treatment. I'll come back in a few minutes."

Mom grinned and waved to the nurse. "Thank you for taking good care of her. Sydney, do you want to try the French toast before they take it away? It's good."

I laughed. "No thanks, Mom. You can have it."

Mom whispered into Grandma's ear. "We'll bring Sydney to visit you soon."

She opened her eyes. "Leaving so early? I miss you, Sydney. Don't forget to come to visit me. I hope I can come home soon so we can talk more. I miss cooking for all of you guys."

I smiled. "That's for sure. Yeah, I miss your cooking, Grandma, especially after school. I pray for you every day. See you later. Love you."

She smiled and carefully lifted her arm to wave goodbye.

Mom held Grandma's hand and kissed her on the forehead. "I'll come to see you during the week when I get a chance. Make sure you speak up if you need something."

I blew Grandma a kiss as I walked out of the room. All the tubes hooked up to Grandma got me worried. "When is Grandma getting out of the nursing home?"

"I'm not sure, but she's getting better, darling." From the sadness in her voice, I knew Mom wasn't telling me everything.

Mom searched all over the parking lot for her car. "I see it now. I thought I parked the car on the other side for some reason. Oh, well."

Grandma had always been my Rock of Gibraltar. She gave me confidence when life got hard. I couldn't have gotten through those years of moving from school to school without her. "I missed having Grandma around the house so much, Mom. We don't laugh as much at home anymore."

Mom grinned. "Yeah. The house is so quiet without her around. I miss the sound of her voice and especially having her at home to talk to about my day. You're right. There is less joy and laughter."

"It looks like we're experiencing the same feelings, Mom. So, it's not only me." My worries melted away whenever I saw Grandma. She greeted me at the door with a hug after school and had something ready to eat—always making me feel loved.

Mom put her arm around my shoulder. "Let's try our best to make life at home feel as normal as possible. Grandma would want us to do just that. We better get going. I'm curious to see how your dad and brother are doing. I left them with a couple of chores to do."

The last time we visited Grandma, I saw her struggling on a walker. She wanted so much to come home, and she talked about how she hated the food. Mom told me the doctors still hadn't told her when she could leave the nursing home. But seeing Grandma out of her bed gave me hope she would be home again.

Chapter 18

What Daryl went through should never have happened. And I didn't want it to happen to anyone again, especially to me or my friends.

The bell rang, and everyone rushed over to the school pick-up area. Michelle usually wanted to go someplace after school on Fridays. "Let's go get ice cream."

I shrugged. "Yeah, ice cream sounds interesting, but how about going to the park to feed the ducks instead? We haven't been there in a while."

Michelle frowned. "I'm not keen on the idea, but it might be fun. You know we don't have anything to feed the ducks with at the park."

"Let's get some popcorn. There's a food mart close by."

Michelle glanced at me. "Is the popcorn for feeding the ducks only?"

You could always count on Michelle to bring up food in a conversation. "It's not just for the ducks. It's for us too, silly." I could smell the fresh popcorn from the food mart as we waited to cross the street.

Michelle rushed over to the counter. "Two popcorns, no butter. Thank you."

I grabbed the bags of popcorn and walked toward the exit.

"Let's go." Michelle just stood there, staring at the hot dogs and burgers on the grill.

She grinned. "The popcorn is making me hungry. I might as well get a hot dog while I'm here. Do you want something, Sydney?"

"No. By the way, when are you not hungry?" I shook my head as she piled on the relish and sauerkraut. The park was only a few blocks from the food mart. As we got closer, the ducks swam toward the rocks near the edge of the pond to greet us.

Michelle hummed nervously. "Here they come. I don't get how they know we have food for them. I guess it's one of those mysteries of life."

I laughed. "Maybe the ducks have X-ray vision and can see right through the bag."

The ducks waddled out of the water, quacking and circling us. Michelle jumped on top of a rock. "Watch out for Mr. Firequacker. He can get nasty sometimes, and here he comes."

"Yeah, I remember him. Better throw Mr. Firequacker some popcorn before he gets upset. You don't want him to nibble off one of your toes." I laughed.

Michelle looked around, eyes darting from side to side. "How am I going to get off this rock? They got me surrounded. I'm trapped."

I shooed the ducks away. "Let's get away from here before they scare you to death." I just loved teasing Michelle sometimes. She looked so silly standing there on top of that rock.

She threw her bag of popcorn at the ducks and made her escape. "I'm not afraid of ducks, but maybe I do have an issue with Mr. Firequacker."

"Are you sure you're all right, Michelle? You know, I've been waiting to talk to you about this idea. Hey, are you listening?"

Michelle pushed her hair back behind her ears. "I'm glad we're far away from those vicious ducks. I never told anyone before, but I have this duck phobia."

I stifled a chuckle. "You're kidding. You should have told me, and we could've done something else."

Michelle looked over her shoulder. "All right, we're in the clear. So, what is this idea you want to tell me? Don't make me pry it out of you."

I chuckled. "No, I'm not going to keep you in suspense. Let's take a walk around the park to make sure your friend Mr. Firequacker isn't around to bother us."

Michelle spun around. "Hey, did I hear a quack?"

"Relax. Mr. Firequacker is nowhere near us. You must be imagining things. Are you ready to listen or not?"

Michelle nodded and smiled. "Yes, please tell me about your idea."

"I want to start a new club at school, and I need your help. I'm confident you know something about how to start one."

Michelle nodded. "What kind of club? Please, provide me with all the details. Otherwise, I might end up giving you the wrong advice."

"Well, when Shawn talked to me about his brother at the school dance, it inspired me. I want to make sure nothing like that happens to anyone again while you and I are here at Winter Garden Middle School. No one has the right to treat another person disrespectfully just because they are a new student or different."

Michelle scrunched her brow. "It looks like you're pretty passionate about this idea. You're an expert for sure when it comes to knowing what it's like being a new kid at school."

I grinned. "Exactly. And it's not a club for new students only but anyone having problems at school—a club where we can find help for students who aren't sure what to do or who to talk to."

Michelle leaned back, looking up. "Let me see if I got what you're envisioning. First, you want a club to help new students like you once were. Second, you want to help students who are getting harassed like you once were. Third, you want to have a place for new students to go to make new friends, who feel miserable eating lunch by themselves, like you once felt."

I chuckled. "Right again. That's a good synopsis, smarty. Are you a mind reader?"

Michelle grinned. "There you go using those big words again. And yes, I am a mind reader."

"Yeah. But what do you think about my idea? Why schools don't have a better way of helping new students adjust is something I don't get." I fidgeted with my hair as I waited for Michelle to tell me what she thought. "Stop keeping me in suspense. Tell me what you think."

Michelle scrunched her face. "Uh-huh, it's a great idea. I know the counselor who's in charge of setting up new clubs at school."

I punched Michelle lightly on the arm. "Great. We can set up activities and have guest speakers, and I know you'll be good at getting the word out and encouraging people to join."

Michelle smiled. "It looks like you already have ideas on how to run the club."

"Yeah. But I want to get all your ideas, too. Try imagining you were a new student, and no matter how hard you tried, the kids at school didn't like you for some reason. I'm sure a lot of students feel this way. It's part of their daily experiences at school. I went through it myself."

Michelle hesitated, then nodded. "Yeah. I never gave it much thought before, but you're right."

I lowered my head. "It would be nice if more people befriended the new students at school. Why do we have to make people feel unwelcomed all the time?"

Michelle nodded. "Well, I never moved much. But I can see how terrible it might feel to be all alone in a new school."

"When I moved from school to school, this was the worst part, feeling nobody cared. Sorry for being so dramatic. You're a great listener sometimes."

"What do you mean by sometimes?"

We both laughed.

"My grandma would tell me Jesus loved the unwanted. I need to be more like Him and reach out to the new kids who are just looking to make a new friend. By the way, thank you for reaching out to me when I first arrived at Winter Garden Middle School. I will never forget what you did."

Michelle cleared her throat. "You don't need to say anything more. I'm convinced. We can talk to the counselor tomorrow."

"Thank you, Michelle. We better catch the next bus home before it gets late."

Michelle stared at me. "I have a request. Let's not feed ducks for a long while."

I smiled. "You got it. We're just in time. Here comes our bus."

Chapter 19

We sat in Mrs. Clark's room at lunch to do some brainstorming on our new club. Students peeked inside now and then as they walked by. I stared at Michelle. "Now that we have the approval to start our new club, what should we do first? I'm counting on you to help me."

Michelle nodded. "Well, we know what the purpose of our club is, right? And we get to use Mrs. Clark's room on Tuesdays and Thursdays at lunchtime."

"Yeah. So far, so good." I'd never done any actual planning for something like this before, so having Michelle help figure things out took a lot of pressure off me. "Where should we start?"

Michelle rested her chin on her palm. "We need to spread the word about our club. It's something called 'marketing.'"

I raised my hand. "Don't we need to recruit club members first?"

Michelle grinned. "I agree. But that's part of the marketing strategy. When we market the club by getting the word out, we're recruiting club members at the same time."

"Smart. You're making a lot of sense." I teased Michelle a lot, but she had good-old-common-sense, as Grandma would say.

Michelle walked over to Mrs. Clark's whiteboard. "Yeah. Now, I need some ideas about how we should proceed."

I shrugged. "Let's make a school intercom announcement."

"I like the idea, but I'm thinking about posting flyers around the school. Let me write these ideas on the board. But since you're going to be the president, I'll let you make the important decisions."

I smiled. "I'm going to be the president?"

Michelle mock-saluted me. "Yes, because I'm nominating you."

I saluted her back. "And you're my vice-president then because I nominate you."

Michelle laughed. "Great. We got that out of the way. Let's now consider the pros and cons of an intercom announcement versus flyers."

I hesitated, then nodded. "I like your idea better. I usually forget about what is announced over the intercom unless I write it down."

Michelle smiled. "Wise decision, Madam President. So, we're going with flyers, and I know you would agree a poster is a must-have as part of our overall marketing strategy."

"I agree we need to have one. And you're right about the flyers. We can post them up around the school. When we pass them out, you and I can talk to the students, letting them ask questions. If we know someone new at school, we can also hand them a flyer to encourage them to join our club."

Michelle high-fived me. "Sure works for me. Students get a chance to know us, and we get to know them."

"Exactly. Do we need to get someone's approval, Madam Vice President?"

"I'll take care of those details, Madam President."

I smiled. "Madam President has a nice ring to it. We made it happen, Michelle. I can't believe it, our very own club to help students. It doesn't get much better than this."

We worked on the flyer over the weekend and came up with the club name and the date of our first meeting. Michelle sketched out the drawings for the club banner and flyer.

"Your sketches look amazing, Michelle. I didn't know you had so much talent to share with the world."

Michelle grinned. "It's nothing. All in a day's work."

*   *   *

Michelle and I got to school early to put up the club banner in front of the cafeteria with the help of the activities counselor. It was weird with no one at school. I stood back to get a better look. "The banner looks great up there."

We danced around and made a silly song out of our club message displayed on the banner, "THE HOSPITALITY CLUB: Chat and Snacks! Come by and make some new friends!"

"I love it," screamed Michelle.

The counselor chuckled. "Congratulations! You guys did a great job. I like what the club is all about. If you guys need help, let me know."

Michelle grabbed her backpack and pulled out a stack of flyers. "What do you want to do with these, Madam President?"

"I know. Let's leave a stack of flyers by the front door of the cafeteria so the students interested can take one and keep some to hand out at lunch. Michelle, we better get going. It's getting late."

As I roamed down the hallway to my locker with Michelle, I heard students whispering about our new club. Some of them even had flyers. "Did you hear, Michelle? Students are talking about our club. So cool."

She fist-pumped. "Yeah, I can't wait to get the word out at lunch. We better run if we want to make it to class on time."

Some of the teachers made a class announcement about our new club, and one teacher even asked me to tell the class about it. I stared at the clock all morning long. The lunch bell rang, and I raced over to my locker and waited for Michelle. "There you are. What took you so long?"

"Someone stopped me in the hallway and asked me about the club," said Michelle, catching her breath. "Let's get going. We don't have a whole lot of time."

I handed her some flyers. "Do your magic, Michelle. Get students to join, especially the new students and the kind-of-new students, too."

"Absolutely. I know who those students are. I'll also ask everyone to invite friends they know to join. Let's remember to smile, Madam President. It's part of a good marketing strategy."

As we split up, I saw Katherine sitting all alone at lunch again. She didn't notice me walking toward her as she munched on her sandwich. I tapped her on the shoulder and smiled. "Hi, Katherine. Can I sit down for a second?"

"Oh, sure." She looked puzzled.

I handed her a flyer. "Well, you know about our new club."

Katherine nodded. "Yeah. I saw the banner when I came to school this morning."

"Would you like to join the club? I think you could help us make sure our new students at Winter Garden are treated right." I didn't tell her what I was thinking, but I figured she would be the best person to make sure students didn't get harassed and bullied.

Katherine drummed her fingers on the table. "All right. I'll think about it. It's on Tuesdays and Thursdays, right?"

"Yeah. I want you to join. See you in class. Hey, invite someone to come along with you." I handled her an extra flyer.

I glanced over and spotted Michelle busily passing out flyers to a group of 7th graders sitting together. She chatted with them for a while, then marched back toward me. "I'm done, starving and ready for lunch. Hey, I noticed you talking to Katherine."

"Yeah, I saw her eating by herself and invited her to join our club. What do you think about having Katherine join us?"

Michelle nodded. "It makes sense you would invite her, and I'm not surprised at all. That's why you're my best friend. Nice gesture indeed, Madam President."

I smiled. "I'll take it as a compliment."

The next couple of days, we prepared for our first club meeting. We worked out what to talk about and the activities we wanted to include to keep the club fun and interesting. I had doubts about whether or not the club would be successful—which I kept to myself.

Chapter 20

Dad heard about my new club and invited me to lunch after school to celebrate. He had a busy work schedule, but he made a point to be home for dinner. I thought this would be the perfect time to get something off my mind.

He pointed to the table in the corner with a window. "I hope you're hungry, darling. Do you want to sit over there?"

I nodded. "Perfect. You know I love corner tables with a view."

Dad asked the waiter for a cup of coffee and glanced up at the lunch specials posted on the wall. He loved coffee so much. "Should I order a pepperoni pizza as usual?"

I grinned. "Yeah. You read my mind. Make it a thick crust. If you want to add one vegetable topping to make it healthier, I'm fine with that too."

Dad laughed. "Are you interested in dessert afterward?" He flipped through the dessert section of the menu.

I nodded. "Maybe we can get something to take home. This restaurant is one of my favorite places to eat. Great pizza and desserts."

Dad placed his hand on my shoulder. "I know, darling. I love this family-owned restaurant. It's got a homey feel to it, and we have some good family memories here to reminisce about."

I cleared my throat. "I'm not sure if this is the right time to bring this up. But I want to say sorry for all the times I disrespected you, Dad. I didn't understand why we needed to move so much. I hated having to make new friends all the time."

He hesitated, then nodded. "Of course, I'm sorry, too. I've been trying my best to make it up to you guys. I didn't want to move either. Those were some of the hardest times for all of us, especially for you, darling."

"I understand better now. You know, every time we moved, Grandma and I had a serious talk in her room, which helped a lot. But it never got easy for me."

Dad cast his eyes down. "Yeah. Again, I'm sorry, Sydney. I don't know if I ever told you, but losing the house your mom loved so much broke my heart. She loved her garden so much. Your mom put a great deal of work into it. But, it made me more determined to get another house for you guys."

I glanced over at the kitchen area where the waitresses picked up their orders. "Is our pizza coming out pretty soon? The smell of food is making me hungry."

Dad took a sipped of his coffee. "They make everything fresh here. That's why it takes a little longer, but it's worth the wait. Sydney, I had a hard time finding work. Those were hard times for all of us and our friends at church. But with prayer, God got us through it."

I nodded. "Yeah. Uncle Harry and Aunt Mary lost their jobs, too. Mom sure loves gardening; there's nothing more she would rather do."

"I made a promise to your mom to get her another house with an even bigger backyard for gardening, but I knew it wouldn't be easy."

"I guess there were a lot of things I didn't understand. Being mad at you all the time was selfish of me."

"Darling, you're not selfish," said Dad. "I was more selfish than you as a kid, and we only moved once growing up."

"Wait. You moved only once. Yay! Here comes the pizza."

"That's right, only one time." Dad peeled off some of the pepperonis from his slice and placed them on mine.

"Thanks, Dad. I love pepperoni. Please pass me the parmesan cheese shaker."

"I was a little bit of a spoiled kid. You've grown up faster compared to me at your age."

I shook the parmesan shaker hard, but only a little came out. "I guess all the moving helped me grow up fast. What do you think?"

"I believe you're right. You're not only more mature but also a lot smarter. Let me help you." Dad unscrewed the shaker lid and poured the parmesan on my pizza.

I pushed my hair away from my face and chomped down on the pizza. "It's so good. So, you think I'm smarter than you. Let me write this down so I can tell Mom you admitted it."

We both laughed.

I pumped my fist in the air. "Mom always told me you're the smartest one in the family."

He smiled. "Well, I think you're going to be the smartest one in the family. You're also better with people, a lot nicer."

I shot back a double-take. "Really? I never considered myself smarter and nicer."

Dad sipped some water and grabbed another slice of pizza. "You're a lot like your grandma in many ways. But you still need to learn to cook like her."

I laughed. "I'm glad I got a chance to tell you what's been on my mind for a while."

Dad rubbed his tummy. "Me too. Maybe we should take some pizza home. We need to leave room for dinner."

"Did you forget? We also need to make room for dessert because we're taking dessert home, right?"

"You got it, darling. It's your celebration." Dad cared and loved me for sure, but the resentment I held on to just made it hard for me to see it sometimes.

"I guess Shawn is part of the reason you started the club. I heard he helps lead the youth ministry. You need to introduce me to him the next time you see him at church."

I grinned. "Of course, I will. You know everything about everything."

"Yeah. Your mom told me the whole story about Shawn and his brother Daryl."

I leaned my elbows on the table, resting my chin in my hands. "Daryl's story inspired me. He reached out with his life to help someone, Dad. The least I could do is reach out to the students who need help at our school."

He paused, then grinned. "I think God is giving you this opportunity to help you grow in faith and love for others."

"Please forgive me. Thank you for all the things you have done for me and all of us. You never have to say sorry again about this—unless you make us move again."

Dad laughed. "I love you more than you know, darling. Sorry again for what I put you through. We're here to stay for a very long time. I promise."

I looked out the window, thinking. "I'm learning a lot about how to reach out to others with our new club and all. Grandma taught me so much about Jesus and how to be more like Him by serving others. I hope she comes home soon."

Dad glanced down at his cup of coffee. "Me too. I hope you know how proud we're of you. I'm going to have another cup of coffee before we head home. We have a few more minutes. By the way, how are you guys promoting the club?"

"There's a bulletin board at school where we can post announcements, and we have a banner and flyers." I pulled out a flyer from my backpack, handing it to Dad.

He nodded. "It's sure an attention-getter. Love the creative design."

"Michelle did all the artsy things. She's talented. Hey, let me read it to you."

All are welcome to the Hospitality Club. New at school, need advice, want to make new friends, join us for lunch every Tuesday and Thursday at noon in Mrs. Clark's classroom, Room A133.

Dad smiled. "What a nice message. You got everything covered, and having the meeting at lunch is a great idea."

"Michelle came up with the idea. I still remember her coming over to introduce herself to me at lunch. She figured this would make it easier for new students to get to know other students and not have to eat lunch by themselves."

Dad nodded. "Who's the president of the club?"

"You're looking at her. Michelle nominated me, and I nominated her to be vice-president. I still need to pick someone to be the club's secretary."

"Oh, I guess I should call you Madam President from now on."

I laughed.

"We should have lunch more often, Madam President. But only if you can find time in your busy schedule. Good luck with your first club meeting, darling. Ready to go home?"

I hugged Dad. "I'll make sure to put you down on my schedule. You got the pizza, and I got the dessert. Let's go home, Dad."

Chapter 21

Michelle glanced at me, smiling. "We're as ready as we'll ever be. We have balloons, drinks, and popcorn. Hey, how about the sign-in sheet?"

"I almost forgot. It's in my backpack. I'm getting nervous, as you can tell."

Michelle grabbed a clipboard, attaching the sign-in sheet to it. "Everything is going to be fine. I'm putting it on the desk by the door. Let's remind everyone to sign in when they enter."

I nodded. "Good idea. Is anyone going to show up?"

Michelle tilted her head. "Of course, someone will show up. Shawn told me he got permission to leave school at lunch to be with us for our grand opening."

"I mean someone other than Shawn." I peeked outside the door again and saw students headed toward our room.

Michelle smiled. "Hey, you guys. Thanks for coming. Please sign in and have some popcorn and drinks."

There were more students than I expected. "I hope we have enough refreshments. We should go around the room and have everyone introduce themselves."

Michelle nodded. "I agree. We should introduce ourselves first. By the way, I got a case of bottled water if we run out of refreshments."

"I'm going introduce myself as Madam President, and then I'll ask you to introduce yourself."

We laughed.

Mrs. Clark's room filled up fast. Michelle did a great job getting everyone to mingle around. I tried my best to remember everyone's name.

I scrunched my face. "Shawn should be here by now. At least Katherine is here to help with the refreshments."

"He'll be here," said Michelle. "Don't worry."

Shawn was a little late, but he gave a great talk about Daryl and how he gave up his life to save another. The students hung on to his every word; there were a few sniffles too. He reminded everyone the school has a dance every year to honor him. The new members opened up about their problems at school. I talked about my experience moving from school to school and how my struggles inspired me to start the Hospitality Club.

Michelle glanced at me, pointing at the clock on the wall. "It's getting late, Madam President. We better wrap things up."

We thanked everyone for coming. Our new club members gave us a standing ovation, which touched my heart. Michelle and I stood by the door and thanked everyone for coming. We got plenty of thanks and hugs as our new club members left. "I hope to see you at our next meeting, and tell your friends."

Katherine rushed over. "I had a good time. If you need me to do something for the next meeting, let me know."

I smiled. "Thanks for coming, Katherine. You were a big help. I'll talk to you later. Bye."

Michelle high-fived me. "Everything went better than I expected. Some awkward silences but not many."

I prayed a silent prayer, then smiled at Michelle. "Yeah. I'm happy our new club members felt comfortable enough to talk about their problems at school. To me, it looked like it made many of them feel better. I'm keeping my fingers crossed that our club becomes their safe place when life at school gets hard."

Michelle erased the whiteboard, then glanced across the room. "We better clean up Mrs. Clark's classroom in time for her class. Remind me next time to ask our club members to help put things away before they leave."

I nodded. "That's for sure. What about the sign-up sheet?"

"I'll take care of it, Madam President. We better get all the trash and don't forget to take down the balloons."

I looked back one last time to make sure the chairs and desks got put back where they belonged. "We're done. We better hurry to class. I still have to go to my locker."

*   *   *

We had a busy week at school, and I needed a break. Michelle called me Saturday morning, asking if I wanted to go for a walk around the neighborhood and maybe get something to eat, of course.

I loved the sound of the birds chirping and the feel of the breeze on my face, especially when I didn't have to hurry to get somewhere in particular. "I'm glad you called. A morning walk is just what the doctor ordered."

Michelle laughed. "It sure looks like everyone is out walking their dogs this morning. Here come your favorite little ones."

The pups spotted me and made a mad dash. I stooped down to greet them. "They're so cute and goofy."

Michelle laughed. "The pups sure like slobbering all over you.

You know, I like having the club. It's a lot of extra work but so much fun and worthwhile too."

We agreed the hard work paid off. Even teachers encouraged the new students to join our club, which was a huge confidence builder. Katherine is now the club's best advocator against bullies. She's known around school as the former bully who stands up against bullying.

Michelle glanced at me. "I noticed something pretty different about you since we started the club."

I shrugged. "Something good or bad?"

Michelle huffed. "Of course, I mean something good. Watch out for this car making a turn."

"You're right. Starting the new club with you has given me more confidence. I learned that reaching out to others is the best way to get your mind off yourself, which I used to do too much of."

Michelle grinned. "Yeah. You did worry a whole lot, especially when I first met you. You worried about your hair, your make-up, your clothes, your classes, your teachers, your shoes, your friends. Should I go on?"

I cocked my head. "I heard enough."

We laughed.

"You know, my grandma once told me Jesus welcomed the unwanted—the lepers, the poor, the sinners. In a way, I believe we're doing something like that."

Michelle nodded. "I heard the story, too. Is your grandma doing better?"

"I don't know. Sometimes my grandma looks better, and other times she looks worse. My mom is always telling me to pray for Grandma, which I do every night. I can't wait until she comes home."

Michelle grinned. "Well, I'm hoping for her to get better soon. I know how much she means to you."

I bowed my head. "I miss having her around the house so much. I wish I could talk to her more and tell her everything about our new club. I think she would be proud to see how I have changed."

Michelle hugged me. "I know she would be proud. I'm even proud."

"Thanks, Michelle. I have so much to thank my grandma for, and I have a lot to thank you for, too."

Michelle smiled. "Yeah. Your grandma will be home before you know it. I bet you guys want life back to normal again."

Chapter 22

I stayed after youth ministry to talk to Shawn. He was busy putting chairs away. I grabbed the Bibles left on the tables and placed them back in the bookcase.

Shawn smiled. "Thanks for helping me, Sydney. So, how is the club going? I wish I could come over more. It's always fun."

"I appreciate all your help with the club. I've been thinking, Shawn. You know, God gave me this club as a way to honor him and help me grow in faith. I'm sure of it now."

Shawn nodded. "God did say we should love Him and love our neighbors, and this is what you're doing. Yeah, you're honoring Him. Absolutely!"

I tapped Shawn's arm. "You're sure filled with God's word today. Let's get some donuts before they're all gone."

"I can go for another donut," said Shawn, rubbing his hands together.

"It's great when someone tells me how our club has helped them."

Shawn glanced at me. "You know, when we reach out to others, it's like God frees us from our pride and selfishness and replaces them with His love instead."

I smiled. "You took the words right out of my mouth. One of my goals for the club is to get everyone to attend church service with me and also to be a part of your youth ministry someday."

Shawn laughed. "If this happens, I going to need plenty of help from you. I'm not going to handle it all on my own."

We heard a knock. Mom peeked in the room. "There you are. I've been looking for you." Before church, Mom mentioned she wanted me to help her in the garden when we got back.

"I have to get going. Talk to you next Sunday."

Mom smiled. "Bye, Shawn. Say hello to your mom and dad for me." We waved and headed down the walkway to the parking lot.

I crawled into the backseat as my brother scooted over. "Dad, I hope you didn't have to wait long."

He grinned. "No, it's fine. I have my cup of coffee along with your brother here to entertain me."

My brother glared at me. "It's longer than I wanted to wait."

Mom put her arm around the edge of the front seat and glanced back. "Shawn is such a nice kid. Did you guys have a nice talk?"

"Yeah. We talked about my club. Mom, God knew the problems I had to go through, with all the moving and all, would help me grow up and make me better somehow."

My brother shrugged. "Your club is all you talk about now."

Mom nodded. "Your dad and I have noticed positive changes in you, darling. It looks like you're focused on helping your fellow students, especially those new to Winter Garden Middle School. You have blossomed into a beautiful young lady at Winter Garden."

I smiled. "Wow! You see that in me. You know, I'm less insecure and less worried about things nowadays."

My brother tapped Dad on the shoulder. "Can we stop to get

some fries and a soda?"

He nodded. "Hah. You're hungry already. I can use a fresh cup of coffee." We filed out of the car and plopped down at our favorite corner booth. Mom and Dad waved at some people from church who were at the restaurant.

Mom looked at me. "Yeah, I agree. I do believe you're more confident, darling. Do you have an idea why this might be the case?"

I hesitated. "Uh, it's because of the challenges I went through."

Mom nodded. "Absolutely. Tough times serve an important purpose in God's plan for you and me."

"I need to remember to see the hard situations in life as God's way to get my attention and make me better somehow."

"Wait. Did I hear what I think I just heard?" Mom stifled a giggle. "What a very mature and insightful observation. You should attend Shawn's youth ministry more often."

We both laughed.

"Sydney, with all the weeds I pull out in the garden, I'm reminded that the difficulties are God's gardening tools used to clean out the weeds in our lives and help us blossom into beautiful people."

I laughed. "I like your gardening analogy. So, you just come up with that?"

"No, your grandma taught me to see the weeds in my garden this way."

"I think you're right. I feel less stressed about things like clothes, make-up, and hairstyles. Is this what you mean by blossoming into a new person?"

Mom smiled. "Yes. Hey, does it mean you're going to stop wearing make-up?"

I did a double-take. "I'm not ready to go that far yet."

Mom chuckled. "I just teasing, darling. We should always thank God for being patient with us."

I glanced over at Dad. "Can I have a slice of cherry pie to go?"

"I guess the donuts at church didn't satisfy your sweet tooth," said Dad. "Sure, I'll order a slice of pie."

"Get ready to say hello again—more people from the church headed our way." I slumped down in my chair.

Mom smiled as they strolled by our booth. "See you next Sunday, and enjoy your weekend."

Dad sipped down the rest of his coffee. "You guys ready to head home? Don't forget to take your pie, Sydney."

*   *   *

Dad veered around a tree branch in front of our house and pulled into the driveway. The winds kicked up again as we climbed out of the car.

Mom locked her arm around mine. "With all the sugar in your system, you should be fueled up to help me in the garden. Let's get changed. I'll meet you in the backyard."

"All right, Mom." I went upstairs and made a stop at Grandma's room. Sometimes after school, I would go into her room to pray. Grandma and I spent a lot of time together in her room laughing and talking, just spending time together.

Dad peeked inside. "Sorry for interrupting, darling. I thought you were in the backyard helping your mom."

"I'm going down in a few minutes." I hurried to my room, changed clothes, and scrambled downstairs.

Mom smiled. "Spending time in Grandma's room again, I see."

Grandma never made it back home. I thanked God for the

time I had with her, and I was grateful for the chance to tell her how much her love and care for me meant, especially during those times when I struggled the most.

I glanced up at Mom. "I miss not having Grandma around, and it hurts so much sometimes. I can still hear her around the house. When will it stop hurting, Mom?"

She leaned forward and stroked my hair. Tears filled Mom's eyes. "Things get better over time, but we never stop missing the people we love. They will always be in our hearts."

We held on to each other, tears flowing. "Love you, Mom."

"Love you, darling, and I still hear Grandma's voice, too. I should get started before the sun sets on us. Maybe we'll do weeding only today. Please get the garden hoe out, and I'll find the special weeding knife I use."

I nodded. "Okay, sounds like a plan. Just tell me where you want me to start."

"I usually find a lot of those pesky weeds around the edges of the garden," said Mom. "Let's start there. I'll tackle the weeds around the base of the flowers."

"Got it!"

Mom paused for a moment, nodding. "The roses we planted are starting to grow in. They're going to look great once they're in full bloom."

I smiled. "Yeah. The red, pink, and white roses blooming all at once are going to look very pretty from the breakfast room for sure."

God answered my prayers and gave me a new life at Winter Garden Middle School and a house with a garden for Mom to enjoy for a long while.

About the Author

Douglas Lim and his wife, Cindy, make their home in California and have been married for over three decades. They are in the empty-nester chapter of their lives. Doug is a family-oriented Christian author and a freelance writer for several Christian websites and publications. He also teaches religious education, volunteers as a chaplain, and serves in various ministries. Doug has a degree in Philosophy and completed Master of Biblical Studies courses in theology and biblical principles. He is inspired by his family and treasures the everyday moments with them.

Other Books by Douglas Lim:
Moments Remembered: A 30-Day Devotional for Families
I'm Scared, Grandpa!

www.ingramcontent.com/pod-product-compliance
Lightning Source LLC
Chambersburg PA
CBHW030819200726
48288CB00004B/1300